What He

Didn't Know

by

Rania Stone

PUBLISHED BY:
Imagine Press Inc.
EBook ISBN: 978-1-927404-58-4
Paperback ISBN: 978-1-927404-56-0
Hardcover ISBN: 978-1-998047-74-1
What He Didn't Know
Previously published as *The Unjustified*
Copyright © 2020 by Rania Stone

Quotes

JUSTICE AND JUDGMENT LIE often a world apart.
- Emmeline Pankhurst, 1858-1928

Justice is good, but it's for the angels. The man cannot endure, he needs mercy. I wonder, my God, if the gate to Heaven is at the bottom of Hell.
- Nikos Kazantzakis, 1883-1957, Greek writer.

Chapter 1

"I wasn't born a murderer—life made me what I am." Nikos Papadopoulos paused, straining to hear a response. When he thought he detected a grunt, he continued. "Can you hear me?" he whispered from where he lay on the dirt floor. "I can't speak louder. They might hear us." He paused again. "I know you're there. I heard you screaming last night. I'm afraid today will be the end for me. They came yesterday to take me to the basement. You were there, too, right? They must have tortured you until you lost your mind, just like me. I need to tell someone why I killed so many people before they execute me." He took a moment, swallowed, and leaned closer to the crack under the door. "There was always a reason. Allow me this confession of a dying man. I promise no one will hear me, and no one will punish us."

He had to speak to someone, feeling this great need as if, in some way, a purification would come, and he would ascend to Heaven. As if the Lord would wash away all of his sins before they killed him.

His legs and hands were bound as punishment after the several times he'd tried to escape. His body was wounded from the electric shocks, and his unwashed hair had become brittle over time. They kept him locked up until they broke him, waiting for the moment when he would speak of what he knew.

What sounded like footsteps approached. He collected himself off the floor and ran to the far corner. They mustn't understand he was trying to communicate with someone else. It was too dangerous. He felt safe after a while and returned to the opening, placing his mouth as close as possible.

Nikos recited what he knew to be the truth as best he could.

I was born in Piraeus thirty-six years ago. My brother, Kostas, was three minutes older. We both had symptoms of addiction since our mother, Kiki, was a drug addict. They kept us in the hospital for weeks until the doctors confirmed we had overcome the danger and no more substances were in our bodies.

We stayed so long that Kiki forgot she gave birth to us and left us there.

Everything feels like a vague dream in my mind, filled with white like the nurses' aprons and smells of alcohol.

We spent the first years of our lives in the corridors of the maternity hospital. The nurses were our mothers, the doctors our fathers, and other children like us were our brothers, our sisters. With each passing day, we grew more jealous of the sick children in the hospital wards because they had parents while we didn't. They felt love and the family's warmth in their rooms, while we didn't. In our dreams, we fooled everyone and went to bed, pretended to be sick, and some of our parents felt sorry for us and took us home with them. That's how we sometimes felt when it was raining, cold, lightning shot through the sky, and when we saw a nightmare, like abandoned pets.

There were new children as well, and because they had nowhere else to go, they were kept there with us for a long time. I remember George was the name of my first friend. He was older than me. The only thing I can recall from his face was a big bruise on his eye. The rest of his appearance is a blur in my mind.

We played and laughed as he became part of our little hospital family. He had told me it was better for him to die than return home. When I asked him what it means to die, he said it's when you feel happy and free, and no one can hurt you anymore. The only problem was that you would never wake up and that you might be in pain a little earlier. I had a question about how I could sleep and never wake up, so I asked a nurse. But as soon as I told her, she seemed scared and brought someone to watch out for George. Then George didn't talk to me anymore. I had told his secret. But I had never understood what it meant to keep a secret before that. Even Kostas was angry with me, and he didn't want George around at all.

Kostas was never interested in taking the first step toward new friendships. He didn't even have to try. Sometimes, it seemed to me that Kostas was so likable; it was as if he had a magnet that drew people to him, even though we looked the same. Our characters were so different. When I met someone, it took me a while to decide whether to talk to them. I've always been hesitant and sometimes distant, and I still am.

Whenever envoys came from public institutions, they agreed that this was not a life for us, closed the door behind them, and never looked back. I once heard that no one wanted us because we were born addicted. I didn't immediately understand what they meant, but I learned it the hard way as I was growing up.

However, we didn't mind that much. Our biggest fear wasn't that we would stay in the hospital until we were eighteen. Our biggest fear was being separated.

Lila, one of the nurses, was the most special of all. She was kind to us. Lila even gave us our names. From her childhood love, she called me Nikos, and my brother was named Kostas, which was her husband's name. We were "the men of her life," and for us, that nurse was as close as we ever had to a mother. She always came a little earlier to see us and play with us. She would bring us sweets, too, and spend her breaks with us. A short, plump woman with brown hair, always caught up in a ponytail. Her cheeks were ruby red, and she had brown, almond-shaped eyes. She was perfect for me.

As we didn't know what it was like to live in a real house, we had to come to terms with living in a hospital in Greece in the early 1970s. It seemed reasonable and, at times, suffocating. Because we were twins, we became the attraction to doctors, which was something we liked.

Every day seemed the same there. The only difference was that they decorated the booths at Christmas; if a child left his toys behind at the hospital, we could keep them. We were delighted for a while in moments like that, forgetting our lonely *real* life.

After so many years, I may not remember many images, but I do remember emotions and smells. I remember when we went out in the courtyard, and we could breathe fresh air. The scent of spring intoxicated my mind, and I dreamed we would leave and do great things one day. We would become pilots and fly over the hospital. We would write messages with our smoke, and the nurses would see them and laugh. That's what we wanted, to make others laugh.

We always had to be calm and obedient to avoid upsetting anyone. Otherwise, there was always the manager's threat that two orphaned children like us would not find someone to take us together, and we would be separated.

As I mentioned, that was the real nightmare.

One day, a little girl named Katerina arrived. I can't remember her face, only her name, and she looked lovely. A police officer had brought her because she had run away from her home. As this was the nearest hospital in the area, the police decided to bring her to us. Like me, she was six years old and afraid to talk to anyone. She had curled up in the corner of her room, continually singing a melody I sometimes still hear in my dreams. Unlike Kostas, I remember wanting to talk to her, who didn't care. When I approached her, the fear in her eyes slowed my step. I took a seat near her, and after some time, she accepted me silently, even though her fear hadn't dissipated.

Then, a nurse entered Katerina's room, bearing food. As the nurse approached her, Katerina screamed, flinching away. Panicked by her screams, the nurse dropped the food on the table and fled the room. I understood what it meant to have a loud voice at that moment.

My brother dove onto his bed and covered his ears to avoid hearing her.

I didn't leave. I remained calm, watching her without saying a word. She eventually calmed down, and I took the plate of food over to her. She must have been starving as she ate greedily, leaving me no time to put new bites on her fork.

After eating, she tried to speak with a voice that seemed to come from the deepest depths of her soul. She thanked me and said nothing more. Until they took her back again, she never left my side, which irritated Kostas—we quarreled over that. It was the first time he had been so angry with me that the nurse had to come and separate us.

I felt horrible when Katerina left, but Kostas was happy because he had his brother back. She returned after a while but looked worse than the last time. Katerina stared at nothing for so many hours. The more I asked her what had happened, the more she closed herself off to me. In the end, when Katerina felt more comfortable, she showed me her legs.

Someone had burned them.

It must have been from a cigarette. She didn't want to tell me who did it, why, or where her family was, and why they brought her here. I didn't know what else to do with her. I wanted to protect her, so I thought about talking to Kostas. He felt that way, too, even though he didn't like her. We swore we would not let anyone hurt her if she told us. Again, she said nothing—just hugged and thanked us.

The three of us were having the best time possible. Katerina was our sister; we were united like a fist until they retook her. Then Katerina was gone.

After a while, she returned once more, and we tried to run away. However, we didn't plan it well. We thought we'd escape from the laundry room, and the rest would be easy. We hid in a basket of dirty sheets. Before the nurse emptied it, we had left the basket and hid in an auxiliary room. We spent the entire night there and heard them looking for us all over the hospital. We were so close to escaping, but Lila's tearful voice stopped us. She shouted our names while crying. Kostas and I had to give up our escape plans. We couldn't hurt Lila like that.

We were beaten due to our escape attempt. Katerina was so angry with us that she didn't want to see or talk to us. The next day, they took her, and we never saw her again. I felt terrible that I had betrayed her, but I swore to myself when I was older, I would correct that.

One day, Lila came into the room with tears in her eyes. She hugged us, kissed our heads, and told us how much she loved us. She explained that the time had come for us to have a real home like all the other children.

Kiki entered the ward timidly. A skinny woman with long brown hair and circles under her eyes was wearing a dark dress that seemed borrowed.

She spread her bony hands to embrace us. We didn't move, standing perfectly still. As she approached, we slipped behind the plump Lila for protection. Lila, who had not yet stopped crying and wiping her eyes, urged us to go to her.

"She's your mommy, your real mother. She was sick, but she's better now, and she came back for you, to take you with her, to be a family." Lila spoke without conviction.

Kostas stepped in front of me like a big brother to see if it was true.

"Mom?" he said.

Kiki hugged him. As soon as she opened her hands, a strange smell came to me, and from that day on, I smelled the odor of cigarettes and alcohol in my daily life.

I didn't want to go. I only knew Lila, and I wanted Lila.

They placed our things in two bags and pushed us into the car that was waiting outside. Lila was crying, and Kiki was pushing me in. I resisted as much as I could, but it wasn't enough. My brother smiled and glanced at me angrily, upset that I wasn't behaving well. I didn't want to leave. The hospital was my home, and I didn't want to be deprived of it because she suddenly remembered she was our mother.

Then there was Katerina. If I left the hospital and she came back, I would never see her again, and then I wouldn't be able to fulfill my promise.

But I had no choice. I was too young to have options, to create alternatives, to be able to define my own life.

Who was it that said adults were the mature ones, capable of shaping the fate of their children?

And wasn't it adults who hurt Katerina?

I didn't trust adults and was about to be proven right.

Chapter 2

THE DRIVER DIDN'T SPEAK. He watched us in the mirror while casually smoking a cigarette. From the beginning, I didn't like how he looked at us—it was hard and indifferent. He was older than Kiki and had a plump mustache. His hair was still black and thick, and he always tried to hide his eyes behind huge glasses like he didn't want us to see where he was looking.

"Guys," Kiki said. "Don't look at him like that. It's not nice."

"I'm Takis, your mom's friend." He spoke in a dry tone. It was the only thing he said the entire way.

We drove a long time as the house was quite far from the hospital. Kostas and I stared out the window in awe as we hadn't gone anywhere. Our life was in the hospital, and maybe a few times, we went to the city close by with special permission. The hospital had a big courtyard with flowers where we went out and played every day. Occasionally, we adopted some stray dogs to remember that we are children, not hospital products. So, this whole journey was magical for us until we got closer to our neighborhood. It seemed like the government and God had abandoned that place.

We turned onto a narrow dirt road full of potholes. It was funny how much we shook with nerves, so we laughed.

Takis gave us a sharp look, and we stopped laughing. Evidently, Uncle Takis didn't like the noise.

The car stopped outside an old house, unpainted with a small, barred door. We went in full of wonder since we didn't expect our home to be externally worse than the hospital.

Outside, curious neighbors had appeared in their doors and windows as if we were the new attraction of the neighborhood circus.

The inside of the house was decrepit. It had one bedroom, a bathroom, a tiny narrow kitchen, and a small living room. In the living room, Takis had placed two mattresses—that was it.

Our new place, our new life began.

We set our things down and explored the house. My brother hugged our mom while I preferred to explore the area.

The old wallpaper had bubbled due to the humidity, and the mold on the ceiling had begun to spread dangerously. Half the bulbs were burned out, but later, when the bills were unpaid and we didn't even have electricity, it wasn't such a big deal. The house smelled of moisture and dust, which was exacerbated by the fact that the shutters were closed continuously. Often, we would go outside to take a deep breath. When it comes to mind, that sick smell still follows me.

In the beginning, everything went quite smoothly. Takis was almost always out, and Kiki was trying to become the mom she never was. She tried to cook with whatever she had. Sometimes, she'd ask for food from the neighbors. They always criticized her while giving her something to eat for us. She would split whatever the neighbors gave her in half and give one half to us and the other to Takis.

I missed Lila so much. Deep down, I was angry that I had lost her because of Kiki. I didn't want her to be my mother; no one had asked if I wanted her. Her scent was cigarettes from top to bottom, and when Takis came, he smelled of whisky.

Takis didn't want us, and we both knew it from the first moment. Kostas told me to talk to him only when necessary and always be polite, as he was terrified of being chased away and losing Kiki. Our mom had learned to obey and be afraid of Takis. I couldn't understand why she was with him in the first place. One day, I asked her where her parents were, and she told me she didn't have any and that she had nowhere to go. Kostas wanted to know where our dad was, but she always changed the subject because she didn't like to discuss it. Once, Kostas asked her persistently, and she burst into tears. He didn't ask her again, as he didn't want to upset her or, worse, lose her.

On the other hand, I didn't care what she did, if she lived or died. She just wasn't enough. Kiki wasn't the mom I wanted to have.

In my opinion, moms lived in well-kept, clean houses. They were honest and affectionate, and they even cooked sweets and cookies. When they spoke, it was sweet, and they didn't cry or squeal. Also, they didn't scream as soon as their children didn't obey something, and most of all, moms didn't beat them. They didn't lock them in the wardrobe just to go somewhere, and men didn't beat them.

I had Kostas as a mom, dad, and brother. I trembled at the thought that someone might separate us. I knew one day I would have to leave him behind. It was a matter of survival.

One day, Takis returned early from his job as a truck driver, and unfortunately, Kiki was out shopping. He told us to serve him food. The pot had only one portion of bean soup, which Kostas had eaten earlier. He became enraged when we explained there was no food and shouted at us.

"Who ate it?" Takis shouted. "Who? Tell me, you bastards. I work my ass off all day and come home to you little bastards eating my food. Who fucking ate it?"

We were paralyzed with fear in the wake of his violent outburst.

I forced myself to move and stepped in front of Kostas. "I'm sorry, Mr. Takis, but I was starving. I couldn't take it anymore without food. Kiki will be home soon and make something for you, too. It won't be long."

Takis smacked his dirty hand on the table so hard that we both jumped.

"Kiki?" he echoed. "After what she has done for you, you still call her Kiki." He jumped to his feet in a rage, then undid his belt from around his thick belly.

I stepped back and bumped into my brother. "She could've just had an abortion. She didn't ask us for our opinion to give birth—"

Takis lunged forward, and my head snapped to the side from the violence of his blow. My cheek burned hot where I'd been hit while my hands clenched in anger at my side.

I kicked him in the knee and ran. Kostas didn't move as I left the house.

I ran like never before, putting as much distance between me and my house as possible. If Takis caught me, I wouldn't survive. I knew he didn't want us every time our eyes met. What I couldn't understand was why he stayed. What kept him in our misery?

I ran through several neighborhoods and then continued farther. What I truly wanted was to leave the slum behind and go back to Lila. Maybe I would find Katerina again. Whatever happened, I didn't want to return to Kiki and Takis. If I returned, I knew I was in for a beating.

Unfortunately, it seemed everything was conspiring against me. Heavy rain broke out, and I had to find a place to hide. My heart felt ready to burst from overuse, fear, and adrenaline. I sat outside the door of a house until the rain stopped. I had nowhere to go, but I wasn't afraid. I still remember how hard the rain fell that day and me wiping my eyes with tears that wouldn't stop. The urge to leave and never return was great, but I couldn't leave Kostas behind.

I sat there until nightfall, knowing it was time to go back. I dragged my feet as if carrying an invisible cross and reached the house. I entered quietly, but the house was empty, and the lights were off.

"Kostas?" I whispered. "Kiki?"

No one answered.

For a moment, I wondered if they vacated the house and left me behind. I ran out to the street and shouted until a neighbor asked me to be quiet.

"Calm down," she said. "What's all the shouting for?"

She stroked my head with her old hands and took me to her house. It was the first time I entered a home other than our own. Although Mrs. Lambia was poor and middle-aged, the room was full of crystal vases, spotless and well-groomed. I looked like I was entering a magical world and had forgotten everything. She made me sit on an old velvet sofa and brought me a glass of water and a spoon sweet.

I hadn't noticed her before, even though she lived across the street. I was forbidden to talk to other people or enter their houses. Mrs. Lambia was quite thin, and I don't remember her face, only the yellow flowers of her dress and her words.

"Your brother is in the hospital," she said, her old voice cracking.

Kiki came back to the house looking for me. When she found me, we went to the hospital together, where I saw Kostas. I had never seen him like that. It was as if a truck had fallen on him.

Kiki told everyone he was hit by a car while looking for me. His face was injured, he had a broken leg, and several ribs were injured. He wasn't talking to anyone, and when I spoke to him, he turned his head away. I will never forget the expression on his battered face.

In a state of absolute silence, and with remorse tormenting me, a few days passed. Takis disappeared, and Kiki stayed with Kostas day and night. Like a smuggled passenger on the family train, I slept curled up in a corner.

Kostas didn't want to talk to me. I shouldn't have left him behind. After a week of silence, when Kiki was away, I reached out to him.

"Please talk to me. At some point, you will have to speak to me. I shouldn't have left you behind. I know now, and I promise I will never do it again."

Kostas angled his face toward me, and he looked me in the eyes for the first time in a week. His injuries, after so many days, were getting better, and his face was taking on its former shape. He smiled broadly. His front teeth were broken.

"I didn't bump into a car or a truck," Kostas mumbled. "I didn't fall and hit myself. As soon as you left, Takis told me we were the same, and it didn't matter which of us would run or pay for it. So, he beat me until I was knocked unconscious. Then I woke up here."

"Takis did this to you?" I looked away briefly to hide my anger. "I will kill him."

"Don't speak such nonsense. Do you have any idea how much bigger he is and how strong he is? You have no hope. Forget about it. You can't change the past."

"I won't forget what he did to you. I always remember those who have wronged me."

Fortunately, Takis had disappeared for a while, and Kiki was trying to find a job. She tolerated him because he gave us money. In return, she gave him a place to stay.

But all that had changed now.

Chapter 3

School started for us, and everything seemed to be going smoothly until a classmate of mine told me what my mother was doing.

Kiki was leaving the house in the evenings. At first, it was only a few hours. Then, it was more. She was completely cut off from us in the mornings as if she was working all night. I was too young to understand what she was doing until several years later.

I could not accept my mother was a prostitute. I didn't want to admit it—I didn't love her.

But Kostas loved her, and that was enough for me.

We had learned to do everything ourselves. We would get up alone in the morning, get ready alone, and leave alone. Kiki was asleep, and when she woke up, she didn't seem to be there. She could sit for hours, lost in her deadpan stare.

Kostas watched out for her. He fed her and washed her dirty clothes that smelled of alcohol.

He often took care of me, too. He acted like an older brother. Although we were the same externally, we were so different. The older we got, the more significant our differences became. I always felt I had a dark side that I didn't want to show anyone.

Only Kostas understood it, and when my mind went to the darkness, he ensured I kept my balance. Most of the time, when he saw me angry, he would speak to me calmly and remind me that the only thing that mattered was that we were together, united like a fist, inseparable.

In my high school years, I got involved with gangs. I was filled with anger and couldn't break it or drive it away. I couldn't deal with the inner turmoil roiling around my consciousness constantly. In no time, I was Fats's right-hand man. No one dared to insult me, challenge me, or mention my mother or my brother.

Kostas was an honor student, the favorite child of the teachers, neighborhood, school, and beloved son of Kiki. In school, the teachers didn't like me, and in my area, they only talked to me when they confused me with my brother.

I didn't get along with Kiki as well. I may not have acknowledged this to others, but it cost me dearly, and that began to show in my appearance, especially as soon as I became a teenager.

I grew long hair to be different from my brother, and I pierced my ear. I dressed as eccentrically as I could to provoke comments. I usually wore black and focused on everything related to death—not because I believed in it, but because it reflected how bad I felt every day.

I started to steal because of Kiki. Whatever money she was making as a prostitute, she spent on drugs, so there was nothing left to us. I immediately started buying food for the house and got new boots with the iron on the front. Kostas quickly got to me.

"Where did you find the money for those boots?" he asked me when he had just returned from school and opened the fridge.

I was sitting at the table, ready to eat a sandwich. I didn't answer him. What could I tell him anyway?

"I asked you something," he shouted.

"Leave me alone," I told him, annoyed.

"From whom did you steal them?" His cheeks were red with rage, his fists clenched. "Speak."

"Are you in the mood for a fight?" I asked. "Why don't you eat something and cut the sermon?" I ate my first bite, indifferent to his anger.

"Are you an idiot? I'm not touching anything. I'm never going to take any of the stolen money. If you want to help, finish high school or get a job. What do you do all day with these bums you hang around with?"

"They are not bums. My friends are none of your fucking business. Who are you? My father?"

"What do you mean it isn't my business? It's just you and me. It will always be my business until I die."

"No one can tell me what to do. I don't need anyone in any way. So, talk to your precious mom, who is wasted again."

"*Our* mother. Can you hear me?" The anger in his voice was quite clear.

"I will never accept her as a mother, and you know it. Go to your whore now."

It was the first time the good Kostas lost his temper and punched me so hard that he knocked me off my chair. We fought on the dirty floor. It was tough to beat him physically because we were the same, but it wasn't my first time fighting. Fighting was my everyday life. Fats told me to hit someone, and then I did it. Simple as that.

When Kostas's face was covered in blood, I stopped. I didn't want to hit him, but he dragged me into this fight. When I realized what I'd done, I helped him to his feet.

"You're not made for this sort of violence," I said. "You're like a woman."

We never talked about it again. We just got over it and continued to live our boring lives.

Kostas always tried for the best in life. I often wanted to make things worse. But I also had evil influences that made me feel like a man while I was still a kid who didn't know what the hell was going on. And yet I felt so strong, so ready to take on the world.

The source of my confidence was Fats. He was a tall, thirty-five-year-old man who was once fat. His real name was Stefano. He didn't feel he could be the big boss with this name, so he changed it to Fats.

From the beginning, he singled me out as he hung around the schools. I was the one who was being bullied by others and was running away to save myself. I often felt Kostas was ashamed of me, and I didn't want to get him involved. I just kept what I was going through to myself as I didn't want to make my life any worse than it already was.

Stefano picked me up one day when the school bullies were beating me. He took good care of me. He came to my aid the next time they tried to do the same. As soon as they saw him, they immediately left. I was amazed at how much power he exerted without lifting a finger.

He lit a cigarette and told me from that day on, I owed him. Of course, he didn't specify how long I would owe him, but it didn't matter because I was under his protection. From that day on, no one dared to mess with me. He trained me to fight in the afternoons. I had to know.

I got the cocaine for Kiki from him. He was the best distributor in the area, and I was close to him. It was only a matter of time before he gave me paid duties. But before he did that, he taught me to steal wallets with quiet and straightforward movements. My hand seemed invisible to the air and gently slipped into other people's pockets. He told me I had a natural talent, and I thought maybe I had taken it from my lost father.

Who knows what kind of guy he was? I often thought about him. Did he know we existed? Did he know we lived like dogs in a forgotten corner of the maternity ward in the hospital?

Did he love Kiki, or was he just one of the men in a long line who just wanted to fuck her?

Chapter 4

THE DAY I FOUND her body was unlike any I've ever lived, before or since.

I felt it when I woke up that morning after a bizarre dream which I couldn't remember. I went to school because I had so many absences. They warned me that I would miss the entire year again if I skipped one more hour of school. I couldn't afford that risk. Whether I liked it or hated it didn't matter. I needed to finish the year out. I couldn't continue to go to high school forever. Also, I couldn't stand being with the little ones who came from junior high school. So, I had to go to class despite being absent-minded and just waiting for the end of the school day.

It was Friday, and I had arranged a bunch of deliveries for the afternoon. I was always consistent at work, as there was no other choice. I knew what happened to those who didn't do their job. I didn't want to end up in the hospital like everyone else did.

Kostas was already in the second grade, and while he was my father at home and school, he avoided me—he didn't want me to spoil his popular, fake image. He pretended to live another life full of family warmth. Always clean and well-groomed at school, he appeared to be coming from a home of an excellent suburban family. Several times, I even caught him taking a different route home to not let his friends know where he lived. He had done quite well to keep the squalor that was our lives a secret. Sometimes, it bothered me, and I wanted to break the glass world he lived in and bring him back to our pathetic reality.

I arrived home first because I always left school like someone chased me. The front door to our humble shithole was cracked and broken. It sat slightly ajar, tilted askew on one hinge. I didn't pay much attention to it—my attention was elsewhere—as I quietly slipped my key back into my pocket and eased it open.

I moved soundlessly through the small entryway, then into the living room.

What lay sprawled out on the floor was something that has stayed with me since that day, like it's engraved, tattooed forever in my memory. No matter how many years have passed since then, I cannot forget it.

Kiki was on the floor. Blood had spilled from the corner of her mouth, and her eyes were dead, her face expressionless. Something akin to terror seized me as I moved closer to her like I was in a zombie state. I didn't touch her body as I fought the urge to hug her.

"Mum?" I whispered, already knowing she was dead.

I could tell someone had choked her from the marks on her neck. I clasped my hands together so tight that the pain my nails caused in each hand helped me suppress the scream that wanted to escape my lips.

I had to keep my nerve. Her killer may still be in our home, and I didn't want to be next.

The living room was a mess. She must have fought with every bit of strength left in her. In that brief moment, while I stood over her dead body, Kiki garnered a new level of respect from me.

As quietly as I could, I moved toward the kitchen. I grabbed an old candlestick from the living room in case someone surprised me. I would aim for the head and hit him hard enough to leave him unconscious for hours. Then, I would tie him up and beat him before handing him over to the authorities.

I was sure it was one of her clients. Who else could it be? Beating that sort of man encouraged me to search every room and every closet. If he were still there, I'd find him, and I'd beat the shit out of him.

In a state of extreme readiness, I entered the kitchen.

It was empty.

The bedroom was next. In the same way, quietly but utterly resolutely, I moved inside Kiki's bedroom.

Uncle Takis was asleep on Kiki's bed, unconscious to the world, baked on drugs or drunk on whisky.

While I watched him in a fury, his eyes fluttered open, then closed. I didn't move or approach him. I waited for him to sleep. I owed it to him. He had it coming—ever since he beat my brother and sent him to the hospital.

I stood with my back to the wall, and I waited. As I was standing there, all the times that I had wanted to kill him came to mind. All the times he hit me, my brother, and Kiki. And now he had succeeded in killing her. He had killed my supposed mother.

My heart raced when I realized I no longer had a supposed mother.

I was an orphan.

I forced the thought from my mind. I needed to stay focused on what I was about to do. I had to finish what Kiki had started.

I found the needle Kiki always hid in the bottom of her red high-heeled boots. I prepared the syringe with a hefty dose of the white stuff and injected it straight into the largest vein in the arm of the half-naked and sleeping Takis.

He was so far gone that he just opened and closed his eyes briefly before falling asleep again. He didn't seem to notice the short, sharp pain in his arm.

I took a cigarette, lit it, and puffed it until the heater at the tip was bright red. I set up his hand properly on the bed, then placed the lit cigarette between his fingers. That was the death he deserved. To die alone on the bed of a prostitute. The one who took care of him fed him, washed him, and was always under his orders—even regarding her will to feed her own children. To die alone, without anyone holding his hand —the hand that used to beat and abuse women and children.

After watching the man who would be dead soon for several moments, I wiped my fingerprints from the syringe, then left through the window after I made sure no one saw me. I decided to make a quick pass from school, so I took my bag and all the money I had collected until that day.

I half walked half jogged to the school so people would see me. I planned to meet up with Fats to have him as an alibi. The police would ask questions, and I would need to have ready answers. When I passed the oft-frequented cafeteria, I greeted all of my acquaintances with a smile as if I were one of the happiest men in the world.

Then I saw Fats, and we discussed a bum on the other side of the street.

I smoked two cigarettes consumed a beer that he'd bought for me, and when he told me a stupid joke, I laughed. In fact, I laughed so hard that, to this day, I haven't laughed like that since. My limbs were shaking as if I had heard the funniest thing I'd ever heard in my entire life.

Everyone has their way of reacting to facts. Some mourn, others weep, some fall apart, while others act angrily. For me, I just wanted to laugh.

The sirens of the fire brigade wailed from afar. I knew where they were going, but I acted surprised. I still remember it like it happened in slow motion: a friend of mine running and shouting at me that my house was on fire.

As if I was someone else, I stopped laughing and took on the most convincing look of surprise. Then I ran toward my house.

I hoped it was all gone, burned down to nothing but cinders and ash.

With great pleasure, which I hid from everyone, I saw that I had succeeded. I was so proud of myself.

Upon arrival, the firefighters saw me and approached. They shook their heads in remorse and told me they couldn't do anything more for the house. They led me over to stand next to my brother, who was crying in despair on the steps of a neighbor's front porch.

I hid my face with my hands, pretending to cry so no one could see I didn't release a tear. Then Kostas hugged me and told me everything would be okay. and we would take care of each other like before. He promised to search for our birth father, and then he collapsed.

As Nikos narrated this through the gap under the door, he felt a knot in his neck.

Sweat covering his body, he got up off the floor, tired of sharing his life in such a way. He paced the room, then set his ear to the door. He was convinced the other person was gagged in the next cell and could not articulate a word. It was important no one listened to him and his secrets would stay safe.

After a while, he stretched and heard bones crack. Then he laid down and continued talking through the crevice.

Chapter 5

W_E _{WERE} _{RELOCATED} _{TO} my favorite neighbor's house, where we stayed for a few days. Mrs. Lambia got temporary permission to take care of us. Public services acted immediately, and thanks to several acquaintances, we managed to spend a few days with her where it was calm. Kostas just lay around Mrs. Lambia's house without saying a word, staring at the ceiling. He didn't want to talk to me—maybe he thought I wouldn't understand him. Well, he would've been right. I never did.

The fire did not completely burn our house down. Most of our things were burned, though. The only thing left to remind us that it used to be our house was the broken entrance door that had turned black.

The police called Mrs. Lambia one day after the fire to see if she would come to the police station and give them a positive ID on Kiki's corpse. She said nothing to us, but we heard her talking on the phone. Kiki's body had escaped the flames. She hadn't burned as I thought she would have, leaving them the option of an autopsy, which they did a few days later.

They found a charred man in the rubble but couldn't identify him immediately. The fact that they found a needle made them think it was for drug use or he had diabetes. Once the authorities finished their investigation, they had an idea of what had happened. Fortunately for me, justice has always moved in slow motion, and besides, I wasn't there then. Of course, I had my mind on the police investigation. I was not afraid of it because Fats properly educated me.

The clouds of depression increasingly covered Kostas. I felt a deep, endless, greedy void. It didn't feel like I was sad because I wasn't actually sad. There was no remorse, no joy, sadness, or redemption. I just didn't feel anything.

Fortunately, we spent a lot of time in our temporary home, and we both felt what a family's warmth was supposed to feel like, what it meant.

Lambia took care of us as if we were her own children. She waited on us with freshly cooked food and a broad smile that offered endless compassion and vast supplies of love.

It was the first time in a long time that I wanted to be a good person.

I was returning to school and attending classes, and I'd cut my ties with Fats. He left me alone for a while, but it only lasted a short time. After the summer exams, when I found out I had failed three classes, he was waiting for me outside the school door.

"You're lost," Fats said. "I understand."

I tried to avoid him, not wanting to have a relationship with him anymore, but he persisted.

Fats gestured toward the school building. "You didn't learn that much in there, did you? How long have we been working together?" When I didn't respond immediately, he added, "Hey, I have a job for you."

"Not interested. Find someone else."

"I'll pretend I didn't hear that."

"Find someone else," I told him as sharply as I could and tried to move around him to leave. But he stepped in front of me and leaned closer until his face was inches from mine.

"I thought you loved your family." He spoke with a sarcastic smile pasted on his lips.

"What does that mean?" My eyes narrowed. "Are you threatening me?" I swallowed involuntarily, moving one more inch closer to him "If you touch anyone in my family, you will have bought a one-way ticket to jail." My heart raced in fear, but I didn't look away.

"You will pay for that," Fats whispered. "Your time will come. You owe me, you little shit."

Fats pivoted on his heels and strode away without looking back.

From that moment, I knew we weren't safe. We had to leave as soon as possible.

I ran home quickly to collect our things. We were all in danger now. He could easily get to us with the connections he had. He would come in the night and hurt us while we slept. The threat was real, and I was scared shitless.

Kostas would come, or I would drag him along with me. Otherwise, Lambia would be in danger, too. I couldn't leave knowing that. Not her, not Mrs. Lambia.

As I stepped inside Mrs. Lambia's house, I saw we had visitors. Social services told us we were so lucky they had found us a foster home. On one hand, I felt massive relief because I wouldn't have to run, but on the other hand, I had a feeling of immense sorrow. I didn't want to leave this house to go to another family. Who knew what problems they would have, and what was the purpose of taking on two new minors in their home? Was it money?

Until then, life had taught me to trust no one, not even myself.

The social services woman had brought several photographs of the excellent family that had accepted to host us until we grew up. The mother's name was Cleo, and the father was George. They had no children of their own and were sponsors for years as parents. With no other options, we gathered our few things with tears in our eyes since the rest burned in the fire, and we went to this new house.

This move meant we had to change schools. We would make a new beginning in our lives, something more pure. At least, that's what I wanted to believe because I felt so dirty after having Kiki in my life.

Sometimes, I felt that I should wash my hands to get rid of the stench.

As if I was Kiki and I had to get rid of my sins.

Chapter 6

A TAXI LEFT US outside the door of our new home in Kaminia. The house was above a bakery. It was clean and tidy and didn't remind us of the hut we had lived in for so many years. It seemed a bit old as if it had come out of a souvenir photo, but at least it was decent compared to the rest of the neighborhood.

Having just arrived and it was still morning, we went straight into the bakery. A well-groomed lady in her sixties wearing a white apron came out from the back to welcome us. She hugged us both forcefully, and it felt like a fog of flour surrounded us. Kostas managed to smile. I was excellent at acting, so I smiled broadly, too.

"I am just so happy to be here," I said. "I hope we'll become a real family under your roof."

Kostas shot me a furious look.

"And you are?" she asked, smiling and satisfied with my fake words.

"My name is Nikos, and the beautiful one here is Kostas."

"If you didn't have hair, I couldn't tell you two apart. So, my distressed children, come and leave your things and get comfortable. Helen," she called over her shoulder. "Come out front for a while. I need you."

Helen popped out from the back.

"Please stay at the counter as I'll be out." She wiped her dirty hands on the apron as she addressed her colleague.

We left the bakery and entered another door that would be our home. We went upstairs, and George, the man of the house, opened the door for us.

"Welcome, my boys. Come, come to our home."

He spoke warmly as he led us to our rooms. I would have my own room for the first time in my life. I thought so, at least. I left my things on the bed as I studied the white-painted room. It resembled a hospital room. It didn't have a housewife's personal touch. I lay down for a while and wondered what my life would be like with these new people.

The only thing that bothered me from my past was the thought that they might learn the truth about me and come to take me before justice.

I gave the highest sentence to Takis because he deserved it, and I felt no remorse. I should have found a way to do it sooner.

The days passed calmly, full of acting from me, silence from Kostas, and kindness from our new family. Social services came a week later to ensure everything was going well and that we had no problems settling in. We made sure everything was fine. After filling in some paperwork, she told us she would come again next month.

As soon as the lady from social services left the dollhouse with the knitted tablecloth, the crystal bowl, the buffet, the expensive dining room, and the renovated cupboards in the kitchen, it got dark.

Mrs. Cleo changed her look. I was almost sure she had become a viper.

"Take your things and go to your brother's room. There's a mattress there. It's time for little Helen to return to her room."

"Little Helen?"

"Yes, my niece. Go and do it now." She spoke with a sadistic smile, an icy mask on her face.

At that moment, I realized that summer would be endless. I gathered my clothes and went to Kostas, who was once again staring at the ceiling.

"Get out of my sight," he whispered.

"Mom sent me. We are rooming together again, like the good old days."

"I want to be alone."

"She told me to come here, that's all. So, here I am."

Kostas got off the bed and approached the door.

I grabbed him by the arm. "Where did all the promises go, huh? Where's the 'I will protect you, and I will be there for you' shit?"

"Passed away."

"What the fuck is wrong with you?"

"I see you smiling and pretending to be happy, and I want to throw up. Cut the crap, at least in front of me."

"Everything I say is true. Speak quieter. I don't want them to hear anything."

"Of course, it's true. Since you're made of shit, you were always like that and will always be. You're such a miserable bastard."

"Shut the fuck up, Kostas. I'm warning you."

"What? Are you going to kill me, too? Will I be next?"

"What do you mean?" I asked, my insides trembling like jelly.

"How did you feel when you killed her?"

"What the fuck are you talking about? I didn't touch your Kiki, I swear. I would never hurt her."

"Tell the bullshit to someone who believes you. Since that day, you're different, and I don't recognize you. You laugh, you're social, you read. You aren't truly like that. So, I've concluded you're trying to hide something."

"I can't believe you." I stumbled back a few steps, then crossed my arms over my chest. "Do you think I'm a murderer? That I killed our own mother? My own blood? What the fuck is wrong with you?"

"You were born that way. It's not your fault, and you're not fooling me. I know this isn't all an act. You're not sorry for her. You have no feelings. Whatever she did was not enough for you. I know you *could* hurt her. I just wish that you could've loved her."

"It's not like that."

"I don't believe you." Kostas crossed his arms now. "Tell me what you know."

"Nothing."

"If I find out for myself and you didn't tell me, I swear to God I'll turn you in." He spoke through clenched teeth, then spun on his heels and left the room.

The truth was, I couldn't fool him, but I had to carry this secret alone. When you have secrets of such importance, you're better off being the only one who knows. Otherwise, things may get more complicated.

Also, I felt sorry for Kiki. I didn't really cry or feel the loss that Kostas experienced, but I felt terrible. I felt sorry for what I could have and won't have. Maybe if, at some point, I found our father, things would have changed.

We slept in the same room. In the morning, before we had a chance to open our eyes, they shoved the door open, turned on the light, and threw two aprons at us.

The happy days were over. We woke up at three in the morning each day to help with the bakery.

These people were looking for workers in exchange for a plate of food and sleep. They didn't want anything else. They were cautious about what they told us while exerting psychological pressure to ensure we complied with their demands.

"Your father, who takes care of you and gives you money, needs you to stay in the bakery until it closes. I assure you, displeasing him would not be wise."

"I can't come to work today," I protested. "I have high blood pressure. If anything happens to me, who knows where you will end up."

Ignoring my words, she said, "Clean the kitchen. I'm an old woman who doesn't care what may or may not happen." She paused to stare at me. "Don't you ever argue with me again. You don't want me to write in the report that you have misbehaved, do you? No one will want you then." She clucked her tongue like she was the king of the world, staring down at me with contempt and disdain. "Do you know how many children I've taken care of? I know what's right for you and what's not."

We had to do everything like good little soldiers and worked non-stop from morning till night. They never trusted us with money, and they always kept someone around to keep an eye on us. In the morning, I made deliveries with a motorbike to all the small groceries in Piraeus, and then I returned to continue working until late afternoon. I spent at least twelve hours every day being a good boy and doing what I was told. How much could I endure to pretend to be good?

In the middle of the sweltering summer, I came across Fats again. I didn't want to talk to him, but he was waiting for me outside a grocery store.

This time, he was holding a knife in his hand.

"We've got unfinished business to deal with." He touched the tip of the blade to my cheek.

"I'm not afraid of you. I'm already dead."

"How about your brother?"

I pushed him away and ran. I couldn't fight or get hurt because I didn't want the attention that would bring.

After a few days, I saw him in front of the store again, and my stomach dropped.

"I want you to do a job for me," he said. "You owe me."

"I owe you nothing."

"I won't play this game with you. You'll do what I say. Otherwise, I'll expose you for who you are, and everyone will know of your achievements." He glared at me, knowing this revelation was disastrous for me.

"Did you forget you've beat people, hospitalized them? How have you muled hundreds of kilos of coke? You have such a selective memory, and you're so comfortable in the role of the unfortunate little boy whose mother died."

"Shut up," I shouted, clenching my fists.

I could attack Fats, beat the shit out of him, but I didn't want Kostas to find out.

That was the only real threat for me.

"Say it," I whispered, unclenching my fists.

"I will give you a package tomorrow. I want you to take it to a drop point north of Athens. It's for rich kids. The contact will be listed and clear."

"Is it clean? Will I have any trouble?"

"Did you ever get in trouble with something I gave you?" He stepped away from me. After a few moments, he shouted back, "You know where."

I felt trapped. I had no choice. All I had to do was go to the northern suburbs and deliver a parcel. This would be the last time, and then I could pretend to be the other Nikos again. The one who was likable, polite, obedient—at least until I was eighteen. Then, I would be free from the system to continue my life as I wanted, to make my own rules, and to cover my needs and beliefs. Things would be different for me if it weren't for the fear of being arrested.

That afternoon, as it was getting dark, I got into a fight with Mrs. Cleo because I told her I couldn't take medicine to her cousin. Instead, I'd arranged to play basketball with the kids from my old neighborhood.

She was quite dismayed, but I didn't leave her any choice. I put on my sportswear clothes, and I went to the stadium. There, behind the bleachers, drug exchanges took place. It was the perfect place where everything was in favor of health and exercise. Fats waited for me, smoking a cigarette.

"You're late," he said, a cloud of smoke encircling his head. "There's a change of plans."

"What change?" I asked.

"We have a rat in our chain somewhere."

"I didn't say anything to anyone."

Fats dragged on his cigarette. "Take the package and hide it."

"I have no place."

"Find a place."

I took the package and put it in my school bag. My intuition warned me that this was all wrong. I went home as fast as I could to find somewhere to hide it.

I couldn't go inside the house because I didn't want to see Kostas, so I decided to go to the bakery and put it in the bag of flour. I would be the first one in the flour bag in the morning so I could take it out the next day.

I removed my T-shirt and entered the house. Our new "mom" was sitting on the couch watching TV. When she saw me, the usual disparaging look crossed her face.

"You're late. Where's your T-shirt?"

"Mrs. Cleo, I was sweating and dripping all over. I'm going to take a shower if that's okay with you."

I rushed away before she could respond. I put the T-shirt in the washing machine with the bakery's aprons.

Someone knocked on the front door. I tried to listen, but I couldn't hear anything.

Before I entered the bathtub, I wrapped a towel around myself and opened the bathroom door to peek out and listen.

It was the police. They were asking for me.

Mrs. Cleo turned my way and pointed, a sneer on her face.

"What happened?" I asked nonchalantly. "Did you learn anything new about my mother?"

"Young man, get dressed and come out here to talk to us."

I stared at them a moment too long, then eased the door closed. I couldn't put my T-shirt back on, so I dressed in my pants, threw the towel on the hook, and exited the bathroom.

They stood in a huddle, muttering to each other by the front door.

My stomach was doing backflips.

The officer moved a few steps closer.

"Young man," the cop said. "Tell us where you hid the package."

When I didn't respond right away, he grabbed my arm and pulled me to the couch.

"I don't understand what you're saying."

"Search him," Mrs. Cleo said, her voice harsh and loud. "Search everything. You have my permission." She pointed at me. "He came without his shirt and went straight to the bathroom. Who knows, maybe he hid whatever was in that backpack he was carrying with him."

Mrs. Cleo sounded genuinely afraid, but I was sure she was happy on the inside. She seemed on a mission to prove that whoever was not her blood had some problem, defect, or flaw. She hated all of the kids she took care of.

With her permission, the policeman searched the entire bathroom, the backpack, the unwashed clothes, and the washed until he put his hand on the washing machine. When he saw the T-shirt, he grabbed it, dabbed his finger on the white powder, and licked it.

"What's this?" he asked.

"Flour. I work in the bakery."

"When did you go to the bakery?" Mrs. Cleo shouted. "You wanted to steal from us?"

Her hysterical voice twisted something inside me, driving me insane. I tried to keep it together so they wouldn't suspect what I was thinking. If only I caught her in my arms at that moment.

I steeled myself and glared at her. "You, Mrs. Cleo, have no love for orphans. If I were your son, you wouldn't behave like a mean prosecutor."

That silenced her for a while.

The policeman glanced between us suspiciously a few times, then signaled to his colleague who had remained near the door.

After the authorities exited the front door, Mrs. Cleo left the front room immediately. She was wise enough not to temper me further.

I was already making plans that a certain someone might have an accident soon. Maybe she would slip into the flour and hit her head. Or a robbery could take place with a tragic outcome. What a loss for the neighborhood. Her fate was prescribed. As for Fats, he'd ratted me out— probably turned into a snitch—which meant he was another one for my list of vengeance.

When everyone was asleep that night, I slipped quietly into the bakery. I had to remove the package. I took a small flashlight to avoid turning on any overhead lights and arousing suspicion of who might be in the bakery at two in the morning.

Like a thief in the night, I approached the bag of flour, opened it, and lifted the package out.

Before I could turn around, all the lights came on, blinding me.

"Police. Drop what you're holding and put your hands over your head."

Chapter 7

I spent the rest of the night in a police cell. My guardians refused a lawyer. Perhaps I deserved that, perhaps not. After a series of short procedures, they took me to a reformatory. I had no voice as I was a minor, and my guardians weren't any help. I will not forget Kostas's face when they arrested me—sadness, frustration, anger.

I had left him alone.

The first day was a nightmare. Fear became my dominant emotion. It had been a long time since I'd felt anything but anger.

The upside was that I could be free to show myself my *real* self in the reformatory. I wouldn't have to pretend. I was tired of that. The time had come for the mask to fall.

They cut my hair, washed me, gave me clothes, and put me in a cell. I remember staring in awe at this abandoned building that would be my home for the next five years.

One particular dark-skinned man about my age wasn't happy to see me. He sized me up for several minutes until I stepped away to check on my things.

He grabbed my arm, stopping me before I got too far, then eyed me down.

I couldn't see his fist, nor did I expect him to punch me in the stomach as hard as he did. I bent over, the air shooting from my lungs.

My guard was down. I was completely unprepared to have my first lesson at the reformatory.

Seconds later, he was above me, one hand holding my mouth, the other clamped onto my neck.

"You'll do as you are told," he whispered in my ear.

I stared into the distance, still trying to collect my breath, offering up a fearful look on my face. That's what he expected, and that's what I gave him. He had to believe I wasn't dangerous.

It took seconds before he released me and turned his back to me. The moment he did, I rushed him from behind and wrapped my arm around his neck, cutting off his airflow. I squeezed as hard as I could while he struggled to escape. His body thrashed under the pressure of my arm, reminding me of a fish dying on the bottom of a boat.

I wanted to end him so bad, but I restrained myself. When he lost consciousness, I hauled him to his bed before the guards came for a walk-through.

Then, a guard approached and saw me standing in front of the door. I had already gotten my rapid breathing under control from the gut punch.

"In a little while, it's afternoon walk time," he said. "Follow the line and do what you are told. Nothing less, nothing more."

The guard moved away from my door.

All I cared about was getting revenge on the bitch who put me there.

I remember staring at the stranger who attacked me. I hadn't decided if I should hurt him further or be patient in case he could be useful later. Luckily, I didn't have to choose as someone shouted over the loudspeakers that the walk was starting.

I tossed water in his face. He got up angrily, arms flailing.

I told him to calm down and pointed at the cell door that had just opened. Then, I got up and joined the line without looking anyone in the eye. I had to find out who the leaders were, and then I would decide whether to talk or not. The sure thing was that I would need an ally because, in places like this, surviving alone would be a challenge.

I felt their looks piercing my back, their whispers echoing in my mind. I was the subject of the day, and I preferred to raise my head only when we went to the yard to avoid the weird looks.

I walked around the perimeter without talking or nodding to anyone. I wanted to check faces and memorize who was with whom. I couldn't risk talking to the wrong person.

However, after observing everyone, I noticed that most people in there were foreigners. I wondered how many Albanians and gypsies knew why they were there, as they didn't speak the language.

Someone approached me from behind, and I spun around, ready to fight.

"Calm down, man." The guy raised his hands high as a sign of peace. "I'm not here to fight with you. You're a fresh fish. You'll need a friend if you want to get out of here alive."

He offered me his hand. I avoided his handshake as I didn't know if he approached me for good or bad.

"I'm Nikos," I said, examining my surroundings.

He lowered his hand and continued to speak.

"You have to learn some rules. Because you have to protect your mind first, then your body. You are only in that cell temporarily. There's over two-hundred-fifty people in this joint. Each cell has a leader, and you have to obey him. Otherwise, you're fucked. Usually, the leader is the oldest in the cell. We have riots almost daily, and staying out of them is good. If not, you'll only achieve an extension of your sentence. Whatever you see or hear, you must never say anything to anybody, no matter what they order you to do. You rat someone out in here, no one will be able to protect you."

"What else should I know?"

He glanced around, then met my gaze. "There are some enemies you should be aware of. The northern Albanians have problems with the south, as well as Sunni Muslims. If some country is at war with another, they immediately separate the inmates. Most are foreigners here. Be careful who you talk to. We have Pakistanis, Afghans, Palestinians, Iraqis, Algerians, Turks, Somalis, Romanians, and many others."

"Thank you for the information, my new friend. Why are you here?"

"Theft."

"What did you do?"

"I stole expensive cars and sold them. Then I got caught, and now I'm paying for it. Once you get in here, time stops for you but continues for all who are on the outside. They'll remember for a while, but the longer you're here, you forget you as if you didn't exist. What about you? Why are you in here?"

"Drugs. They trapped me."

"Brother, you're talking to me. This isn't a courtroom."

I closed my eyes briefly without responding.

"We'll talk later," he said and strode away.

The truth is that I liked him.

I glanced around the yard, wondering if there was any chance of escape. There were high walls, barbed-wire fences atop those walls, and armed guards.

I came to my senses. I couldn't risk an escape on my own. But what if I had an accomplice?

With these things on my mind, time passed, and we had to go back inside. They didn't put me in the cell with my attacker again. They even changed my floor.

There was a bad smell coming from the prison cells on this level. They were decorated with various flags and symbols, depending on their nationality. When I entered my new cell, I avoided eye contact with the three guys watching me as I didn't want to fight.

"The top bed is yours," one of them told me.

He didn't seem to fit the environment. Blonde, with a thin nose and a pair of black glasses.

"I'm Peter, the leader," he said.

I told them my name and then set my things on the bed. There was no place to sit, so I hopped up and sat on my bed.

"His name is Monk, and the other is Sheeran," he added. "Sheeran has been our singer for a long time, and the Monk shows us the way of God."

He talked as if we were at some reunion of old classmates.

"Well, Nikos, why are you here?"

"Drugs. You?"

"My reason is better. I organized improvised car races, continuous obstruction of transport, dangerous driving, exceeding speed limits, and causing physical damage, or as they call it, public mischief."

"That's why you're in?"

"If my parents wanted to pay, I wouldn't be here. This was a lesson, they said."

"How much was your sentence?"

"Three years. My sentence was longer because of the gambling. I had made a lot of money the night I was arrested. Unfortunately, they confiscated everything from me. The cops shared the money with each other."

"Sheeran?"

"Drugs."

"Using or selling?"

"Both."

"And now?"

"There's no way out. I've made peace with it and came out a winner. Now all I have to do is hold on, not roll over again."

"What do you mean?" I whispered through my teeth.

"Everything happens if you have the right tools."

A guard passed by our cell. Monk was holding a rosary, playing with it in his fingers. He didn't say a word to us; he just continued whispering prayers. He must have lost it.

With this company in the cell, the first week passed almost quickly. Peter and I spent most of our days together while he informed me about everything. He had already explained the jail's cliques and began telling me stories of my roommates.

Sheeran, or John, came from a low-income family of refugees. Among them were his grandparents. The settlement he'd been living in was gradually abandoned, and its inhabitants were foreigners working in the fields. Sheeran was hoping for a better life, having lost his father to cancer.

His lust for easy money had him selling hashish to immigrants who lived thirty to a room. When they ran out of money, he moved on to new customers and was unlucky enough to try to sell to the son of a police officer.

Monk, or Stefano, was complicated. This was the typical case of how one can ruin his life by messing with the wrong people. He came from a profoundly religious family. He always behaved according to the Gospel. He was tired of being the sheep of the class and everyone teasing him non-stop. He was taught that he must turn the other cheek when someone hurts him. How he must forgive, not curse, come home early, and never deviate from the path of God.

And he did so until he met Constantine. Gradually, he began to make Monk question the way of life he was following. He showed him excerpts from books about black magic and the worship of Satan. Monk tried to avoid him at first, but Constantine offered him something hard to resist at that stage of his life. Constantine was older than him. He'd already finished high school and knew how to care for himself. When Monk was with Constantine, he felt important because girls paid attention to him. He used to be invisible, but now they invited him to all the parties. Without realizing it, he followed Constantine faithfully and did whatever he told him to do.

Then he met Lina, a gorgeous girl. Lina seemed interested in him, and Stefano lost his mind with her. She persuaded him to read Tarot cards one day, explaining that this was white magic. The cards showed him that he must trust her and be with her. He was so deeply in love and had thoughts of marriage. Lina talked about their love being blessed by her church. Stefano hesitated, but he decided to accept the blessing ceremony since he wanted her so much.

They drove at night to ancient Corinth, an old government building that had been abandoned for many years. Everything was prepared for the couple. Wearing a black hooded cloak, Constantine was waiting for them. Candles were everywhere, with some forming a large pentacle at the center.

Constantine had begun to recite some verses, and Lina smiled as she slowly disrobed. Naked now, she laid in the center pentagram.

Constantine had taken a candle and was burning a rosary around her. Then, he seemed to ask Satan to give him money and fame and put a coin on Lina's forehead.

Next, he lowered himself onto Lina and entered her with passion.

Stefano recited that watching Constantine fuck Lina like that was the most shocking thing he had ever seen in his life. Then it was his turn to fuck his heart's chosen. Lina urged him to take her, but Stefano hesitated until Constantine insisted. Unsure of what was actually going on, as if in a daze, Stefano got down and laid with Lina.

While Stefano was on top of her, Constantine muttered hymns and threw wheat around them. Lina closed his eyes, and Stefano surrendered to her.

He felt helpless, the ability to refuse lost to him as he thrust inside Lina, over and over again.

A squeal of some sort startled him. When he opened his eyes and looked at Constantine, the man held a slaughtered rooster. With the blood from the rooster, he bathed Lina.

Stefano was so frightened he pulled out of her and got to his feet. They fought, with Stefano telling them he didn't want to have any relationship with either of them.

When Constantine threatened to tell his parents, Stefano mellowed.

Similar ceremonies with Lina followed. She was the Priestess of Satan, and Constantine was the High Priest. Without realizing it, he found himself embroiled in a cult. He blindly followed Constantine and Lina and did whatever they told him. He was a puppet in their hands, unable to free himself from the black shackles.

They were trying to convert more and more young people to the worship of Satan. In each ceremony, there was a lot of sex, and Stefano found himself enjoying it so much, being wanted and accepted. He was the happiest he could be but was falling into a trap. Whenever they were asking for something, they were sacrificing an animal. The more they wanted, the larger the sacrifice.

It was only a matter of time before they committed a crime in Satan's name. Under the pretext of white magic, they led a new girl to a deserted location, and after they stripped her, they knocked her out and strangled her.

Afterward, they violated her lifeless body, covered her with gasoline, and then burned her to erase the evidence.

Ordinary Stefano, God-fearing Stefano, had become a Satanist and a murderer. After a while, they committed a second crime. This time, they chose the victim by chance. When the police found their tracks and his parents learned the truth, he seemed relieved. He confessed everything and since then has tried to find forgiveness through the church. He prayed for himself and the souls of the women he had killed.

Peter had a more straightforward story. He was an ill-educated suburban child who didn't know how to kill his time. Having everything he needed in life, he got any girl he wanted, went to the most expensive places, had a collection of sports cars, and whenever he got bored, he had big parties where alcohol and drugs played a dominant role in the fun.

After a while, he started organizing car races. The police knew and arrested him several times, but he always got out of trouble because of his wealthy parents. The last time, however, he was drunk; he had also used drugs, and his parents decided to teach him a lesson.

These were their stories, but I didn't care how it happened to them or why. Everyone had a cross to bear. My problem was different. I was tired of all this pretending, trying to hide my dark side. I knew I had to be a role model to get out early and say that I regretted what I'd done and would not do it again. I would tell them I wanted to start school again in September. I also had to be willing to participate in all of the reformatory activities to show everyone how I was being reformed. In the few meetings with experts, I said I wanted to be useful in society and that when I got out, I would get a job.

When they asked me how I see myself after ten years, I said what they wanted to hear. I said I wanted to be a family man with two children and a good job. That's what they thought was normal for me. But the reality was quite different.

Peter left the jail after his saddened parents got him out. But he didn't forget me. He sent me drugs through a guard so I could make money in prison. We were both winners. I didn't bother anyone and did things for those I thought could repay me.

Most importantly, I didn't do drugs.

My first plan upon leaving the reformatory was to find Katerina.

I also wanted to stay away from this stranglehold with my brother.

My second plan was to get some revenge on Mrs. Cleo, to burn her as I burned Takis. She had to pay for what she did—and was still doing—to orphans.

If there wasn't justice, there was me.

Sometimes, in my sleep, I could hear Takis screaming and see his burned face.

Then I saw Kiki covered in blood, shouting, "Justice" repeatedly at me.

Is justice out there? How about for someone like me?

Is there justice for someone like Kiki?

Chapter 8

I WILL NEVER FORGET the day the northern Albanians bribed a guard so he would let them do what they wanted. Three of them came to my cell. I was alone as they'd arranged for my cellmates to be gone.

I'm always friendly, and when I got off my bunk and asked them what was going on, they jumped me. Two of them held me, and the third one drove punches into my gut.

My ability to resist three attackers was greatly hindered, and they beat me badly. Then they removed my clothes, but that was as far as they got because Sheeran stepped back inside the cell. He shouted at the guards, and the Albanians ran, leaving me naked and covered in blood.

The pain was unbearable. I had never been beaten that bad—I thought I would die. I was sure I would've been raped if Sheeran hadn't come.

They didn't want me to give drugs to the Southern Albanians. They only wanted me to provide to them, and only if the Southern wanted they would make the sale.

I was taken to the infirmary, but the authorities didn't notify anyone. They tried to keep the incident secret as it was not the time for scandals.

They gave me heavy drugs to manage the pain. In those moments, I needed Kostas more than ever. I wish he knew what was happening. To be able to see him for a visit would have meant the world to me.

However, they didn't allow it. And as a minor, he wouldn't have been able to come alone.

When I finally opened my eyes in the infirmary, someone was in the bed next to me. His head was wrapped in gauze, and he stared at me in astonishment.

"What did they do to you?" he asked.

"Isn't it obvious?"

"I'm George. At least that's what they told me, although I don't remember anything."

"You don't remember anything?" I whispered. "That must be weird."

"I was told I would be transferred from the jail where I was. Of course, I don't remember why I was there."

"No one goes there accidentally."

"I wish I could remember, but whenever I try to remember something, I get an unbearable headache that blocks everything. I only have scattered images in my mind, and I can't connect them. Imagine for a second you were a vast puzzle, and all of your pieces dissolved in the air. You stand and look at the catastrophe as it hovers in slow motion. Sometimes the pieces look alike, and sometimes they seem entirely unrelated to each other."

"It could be redemptive. I wish something like that would happen so I could start from scratch like an unwritten book or an untouched painting."

"It's so hard to know if someone's telling you the truth or if they just want to take advantage of you. Some people simply want to make fun of you."

When the nurse came in, George stopped talking. She came straight to me, not paying George any attention.

"I put painkillers in your serum to keep you going. Hopefully, now you can sleep."

"Nurse," George muttered. "Are we going to eat anything?"

She didn't give him the slightest attention as she left the room.

"Nobody cares about me," he whispered.

Then I fell asleep. When I woke, George wasn't there. Instead, the director of the prison was sitting on his bed.

"My child, how are you?"

"Good."

"I need you to tell me what happened."

I shook my head. "If I speak to you, I'll be known as a rat. My life will be forfeit."

"I will offer you assurances that will not happen."

"With all due respect, it's not in your hands."

"I want names. I know my guards were involved."

"If I give you names, they'll make my life miserable." I glanced toward the barred window. "I still have a long way to go."

"If you tell me who's responsible, I'll work on getting you out of here faster."

"I'm sorry, I can't help."

If I were to speak, I would have to say that I was the one who trafficked drugs in prison.

The medicine they gave me was quite heavy on my system, and I was always asleep. The next time I opened my eyes, George was there again.

He smiled at me. "I'm getting better and better. Of course, my memory has not returned, but I'm almost okay, according to them. When do you go out?"

I tried to sit up, but the pain held me back. "I don't know. But let me tell you, I don't want to go back there." I had just woken up and was already tired.

"Why would anyone want to?" he asked, staring at me as if I'd said something stupid.

But then I fell asleep again.

The days passed in a blur, and I only thought about revenge. I knew my attackers, and they'd been ordered to beat me. The one who threw the punches was Roberto, a notorious knife killer. He was imprisoned for murder. The guy was always involved in quarrels and somehow got away with it.

The other was Dori. He was in the reformatory because he wouldn't rat out his gang, who were thieves. The last one was Andreas, who had gotten caught up in a clash between police and some looters. That wasn't a serious reason to be in the juvenile detention facility, but he didn't have the right papers. After some time and a little reformatory education, Andreas became like the rest of us.

I wanted to kill Dori first. He was the weakest of the three. Andreas would be next, and then I'd let Roberto know, and he would wait for his turn. I would find a way to torture him because sometimes the waiting is equivalent to Hell.

I made the mistake, in a sleepy stupor, of telling George that I was just thinking of revenge.

"Why would you want to do that?" George said. "You're asking for trouble. Let it go, and concentrate on doing your time. Then you'll be free. You'll have all the time you want to get revenge once you're on the outside."

I already regretted telling him, but a part of me knew he was right. The next day, he left, and two days later, I was released from the infirmary.

Sheeran and Monk were waiting for me in the cell.

"There you are, beast," Sheeran said, lightly wrapping his arms around me and slapping my back.

"I don't know where I'd be without you," I whispered into his neck. "I owe you."

He released me and pushed me back to arm's length, staring into my eyes. "You'd do the same for me."

Would I do the same for him? I wasn't so sure. I'd only ever felt anything for a few people—my brother, Katerina, Lila, and my neighbor. The rest just existed next to me, like shadows. Every day was a battle to appear happy, approachable, and friendly.

My mask never fell.

The days passed, and I made my plan. I decided I wouldn't sell my product to the northern Albanians again. I reached out to the southern Albanians. I knew their leader. They called him Renato. We had a chat, and we agreed on a deal. I would sell him and his people any quantity he wanted at the best prices in the joint, but it came with one single term.

He would arrange to have my three attackers killed in the order and in the way I wanted.

One day, Dori received a package. He opened it, and inside was another package, and within the other package, there was another. He unwrapped them all until he got to a small box wrapped in a red ribbon. Inside that box was a photo of his little brother. On the back of the picture, it read 13:30. That was the time when the inmates went for lunch.

He didn't know what to expect. Like a wild beast in a cage, Dori paced the cell non-stop until the others found him. He didn't tell anyone about the photo.

When it was time to leave the cell for lunch, his nerves were rattled.

One of the prisoners in front of him pushed another, and there was a small commotion. Then, someone slipped something in his pocket. He glanced around to see who it was but couldn't tell. He was dying to look at what was in his pocket, but he knew he couldn't yet. If the guards saw him pull something from his pocket, they'd take it from him.

He walked with the others until they gave him his portion of food, and then he sat alone at a table. He placed a hand in his pocket and touched what felt like a bottle. He unrolled a small piece of paper attached to it from around the bottle with an elastic. The word "DORI" was written in Latin characters.

I watched him from the other end of the lunchroom. Dori trembled when he read what was on the paper. I wanted to see him suffer, to know he was marked for death. There was no way he could connect me with the message.

Dori crossed his fingers and whispered something to himself. He knew this kind of message in jail was real.

Someone wanted him dead.

If he didn't die, his brother would die in his place. Dori couldn't let that happen. His family wouldn't stand for it. His younger brother was their only hope that they could be proud of a son. He read, studied, went to school, and helped at home. He was their good son, the good brother. They had already told Dori that he was dead to them and, when free, to not look for them.

Dori stared at the bottle, his lunch untouched in front of him. After a moment, he uncapped it, placed the bottle to his lips, and drank the contents in one gulp.

Then he sat still and waited. It didn't take long for it to act. I had learned about that poison. Once it entered your system, it didn't let the cells breathe.

Dori slipped off his seat and convulsed on the floor. The guards ran toward him as the din in the room rose to commotion levels.

One brother dropped to his knees to help, and a nurse arrived. They tried hard to get Dori on his side so if he vomited, he wouldn't aspirate the bile into his lungs or bite his tongue.

A few minutes later, Dori was dead. They removed his body from the lunchroom in short order.

Everyone was there to see it, everyone watched.

Andreas was next.

We also repeated the same scenario with him, except for a small change. He received a small box with a recent photo of a loved one. He located his bottle of poison in a pocket as well.

But he didn't drink it, as I suspected he wouldn't.

He got up on a chair in the lunchroom and shouted, "I'm not afraid of you!"

Then he upended the bottle of brown water and poured it on the table beside his lunch, making a show of it.

Everyone knew he was the next target now. The guards returned him to his cell and left him alone to think about his lunchroom antics.

Roberto scanned the lunchroom, fearing he might be next. He was next, but not too soon—I wouldn't do him the favor. The expectation of death had to eat at him every night, depriving him of sleep, always looking over his shoulder, afraid to eat.

When I returned to my cell that day, a surprise awaited me.

George was there.

"What are you doing here?"

"Did you exact the revenge you wanted?"

I looked him up and down and decided to answer. "Almost. I've reached the end. For now."

"Why are you doing this?"

"I'm doing nothing. Others do it for me."

"You're enjoying it, aren't you?"

I thought about that for a moment. "I assumed when it happened that I'd feel better, but I've realized that once you've endured horrible things, nothing can compensate you, not even revenge."

"Then stop what you're doing. End it."

"Everything's arranged now." I smiled. "It's too late."

"When there is a will, there is a way."

"No one will miss him."

"You don't know that."

I shrugged. "When someone comes after me, I hurt them back worse. There are always consequences."

"What are the consequences?"

"Whatever I decide."

"And who appointed you judge and jury?"

"Me." I smiled again, but it was more of a smirk this time.

"And what makes you think you're right?"

"My sense of justice is enough for me. If you do something wrong, you pay. That's it."

George suppressed a laugh. A guffaw slipped out, though. "There's a huge difference between beating someone and killing someone."

"Their fault—they drew first. Tell me, why are you here? Because this discussion is getting annoying."

"The others are coming," he said, jumping into the upper bunk.

George managed to ruin my mood. He made me think things I didn't want to. Maybe his goal was to torment me. If I didn't think I'd need him later, I'd get rid of him, as there was no need for his stupid comments.

Monk showed up and glared at me. "You must confess your sins," he told me.

"I have nothing to say to you, especially with George in the upper bunk. And I don't believe in the salvation of the soul."

"Did I hear my name?" George asked.

"Don't interfere," I snapped at George, my tone harsh.

Monk moved closer. "You have to excise the darkness before it consumes you. Something's wrong with you."

"My friend, the darkness, and I are one. I don't have to do anything, and I don't want to. I love who I am."

"You're sick, Nikos. You're the one who's hiding behind the murders." Monk's voice rose as he spoke.

"You're wrong."

"I don't think so. The darkness has not only taken your soul. It's eating your mind, too. You have to repent and get back to God's way. Only then shall you find the peace you seek."

"The guy has a great imagination," George muttered above us.

"Hey, Monk, leave me alone. I don't bother you with—"

Monk moved to one foot away and crossed himself. "I believe in one God, our Father, the Son, and the Holy Ghost."

He moved so close I backed away from him.

"Are you completely crazy?" I shouted, but Monk continued to pray.

He even tried clinging a hand over my mouth to forcefully shut down my protests.

"George, get him off me."

George laughed. "What's the worst he can do to you?"

"Light from light," Monk said, holding my mouth now and using his body weight to immobilize me.

I couldn't take anymore. I bit into his finger, drawing blood, which spilled into my mouth and onto my lips.

He jumped off me, screaming in pain.

Guards came at once.

"What's going on in here?" they shouted.

Once they assessed the situation, the guards placed me in solitary confinement. Monk cried out that I was possessed. Only God could save me now, he claimed.

I spent the next few days in solitary confinement. In the endless loneliness, I was left without a book, a light, or even an hour of exercise. Nothing, day after day, but four walls and the prison of my own mind.

I thought about my brother and how I'd like to see Kostas. I know he hadn't forgotten me. Mrs. Cleo would stop him. She wouldn't let him talk to me. Not even one call.

How could I take revenge on her without hurting my brother? I would do it to her and Fats at some point.

Then I thought about how I wanted to find Katerina. Only she could understand—only her. But where would she be? What happened to her? I could still recall the song she murmured when she felt terrible. I'd love to find, hug, and show her how I'd grown up and how strong I was. I wouldn't allow anyone to bother her, and those who had hurt her—well, we'd find a way to get our revenge.

Everyone would pay for what they'd done to us.

Bodies would line the streets, and then we'd be happy.

We'd live together, broke but happy.

Chapter 9

After solitary confinement, they changed my cell and put me in a cell with crazy junkies. They used to be regular customers, and every conversation with them was a waste of time. I had left the drug business behind and told Peter I didn't want to do it anymore. I gave his contact to the southern Albanians.

The junkies told me that after Andreas put on a big show of pouring the poison out on the table in the lunchroom, the guards discovered it wasn't poison after all. This was something I knew as that was the plan from the start.

They told me that Andreas was dead two nights later.

Guards found him in his cell, an empty bottle of poison on the floor beside him, his throat and insides eaten out by the acid—or whatever was inside that tiny vessel.

I also learned that Roberto was dead. He was found in his cell, lying in a pool of his own vomit.

My revenge was complete and successful.

The police were investigating. Interrogations had started with the immigrants first and then the rest of us. At some point, they called me to the main office. Even though an investigation was underway, all suspicion was gone from my head due to my being in solitary confinement when Andreas and Roberto were murdered.

"Nikos?" One of the officers stared at me.

"Yes." I acted unsure of myself, like I was afraid to be there.

"Did you know the victims?"

"What do I have to do with Albanians?" I asked as if the question had insulted me.

With graying hair and thick fingers, the middle-aged policeman narrowed his eyes. "Please answer the question."

"No."

"Some time ago, you were beaten."

"Correct."

"But you didn't give up any names."

"No one gives names here. It's enough that I was beaten once. I didn't want to experience it a second time."

"Before we finish …" He grabbed my arm, leaned closer to my ear, and said, "You have greetings from Kostas. He cannot contact you, but he hasn't forgotten you."

I eased back, surprised at what I'd heard. "But how?" I whispered.

The door shot open. I couldn't get an answer. Another policeman entered and nodded at him. Then they took me back to my cell.

On that same day, they took Harris from the reformatory and transferred him to an adult facility until new charges were prepared and brought against him. They found empty bottles under his mattress—bottles like the poisonous ones.

I don't know why they blamed him. We hadn't agreed on such a thing. With murder charges, he would never get out of prison, and he didn't deserve it. He was the first to help me when I entered the reformatory. It was a collateral loss, and I would've blamed him if I had time to save Roberto. But Monk losing his shit wasn't planned. You can't plan what fate awaits you as much as you try. Something will always work at overturning your plans. Those are moments where you can show how adaptable you are.

The day I turned eighteen, I had a visit. It was the first after so long. The only ones who came to see me were social workers, psychologists, and doctors. Curious, I shuffled to the visiting room. Because of my excellent behavior, I was escorted without handcuffs.

When I opened the door, Kostas was sitting in the visitor room.

"My brother!" I shouted at him and then hugged him tight I couldn't remember the last time I felt anything other than hate. Everyday life was filled with it, my mask black.

But I felt such joy on that day.

"Nikos, how are you?" Kostas took a seat. "You've lost some weight." He studied me for a moment. "It's hard to get used to short hair. I feel like I'm looking at myself in the mirror, but you're thinner."

"Where were you?"

"Because we were minors, they didn't allow me to come to see you without my guardian's consent. But today, we have a birthday. I don't need anyone's permission anymore."

"You couldn't call?"

"My boy, I did call you, but they never brought you to the phone. Mrs. Cleo had given specific instructions not to bring you to the phone because she thought you were mentally ill and ruining anyone communicating with you. But I managed."

"Yes, the cop conveyed your message. Where did you find him?"

"He's a neighbor. I went to his mother's house with bread every day. Then we met, and I told him our story. He was sorry and said to me that he would talk to you at the first opportunity. Then, after we talked some more, he convinced me."

"Convinced you of what?"

"To become a police officer. I've already done the examinations."

"Did you become a cop?"

"Not yet, but I went to school."

"Wow. Well done. In here, you know what they say about the cops, eh?"

"Yes, but you don't have to remind me."

"My brother is a cop." I shook my head back and forth, staring at him.

"There's something I need from you."

"From me?"

Kostas nodded. "I need you to be a role model."

"In here?"

"Yes."

"Why's that?"

"I want to get you out of here. It will take me a while, though. I have some connections, and I want to clean your record. I want you to get out of this mess and start fresh. That's what I wish for you, and then we can be together."

"That sounds great." I smiled so wide that I thought all my teeth were showing. "Thanks, bro."

"I don't want you to thank me. I want you to promise me."

"Promise you what?"

"I want you to promise me you'll put aside any revenge plans." He stared into my eyes.

It felt like I was seeing the best side of myself talking to me.

I opened my mouth, and he raised a hand. "Don't say anything. Just promise me you'll let go of all the memories that still haunt you as long as you're here. And I promise I will get you out of here and help you stand on your feet again. Also, at some point, maybe you could forgive me and Kiki, too."

A guard stepped in to tell us that the visit was over.

I left the room, my eyes fixed on my brother until the door closed, cutting off my view. I missed him so much. Every day, I felt like I was missing something, a piece of me. Now that I had seen him, I felt whole again.

But what he asked me was so hard. How could I let everything go? Mrs. Cleo and Fats, who had set me up because I wanted to escape him? And Kiki? How could I forgive her? The woman who was supposed to be our mother, the only person in the world who would give us love. Yet she had abandoned us, and when she took us back, she was nothing but a hollowed-out fossil, a shadow of what she could have been.

Nevertheless, it didn't matter anymore.

My mother was dead.

And so would the others.

Chapter 10

IT TOOK MONTHS FOR my brother to get me out of the reformatory. In his letters, he gave me courage. I had to discipline myself. Freedom was more necessary than revenge, and I did what I was told for whatever reason. I didn't have a choice. I buried my darkest emotions as deeply as possible and was patient. With purpose, I could endure anything.

One day, the director called me to his office. He told me my release documents had arrived. It was time for me to leave, but it wouldn't be that simple—it was never easy for me.

A soldier entered the room. "Lieutenant Spyros." He greeted me with a military salute.

Without thinking, I got up and reciprocated the greeting.

"Nikos, we need you to come to the camp for a job."

"A job?"

"I have recommendations from the central police that you are the perfect candidate."

"I don't understand," I said.

Spyros nodded at the others, and they left the room.

"I need someone who's patient and motivated to get the job done right. I don't want a Boy Scout. I need someone who's tough."

"What exactly do you need to be done?"

"I want you to go to the camp in Evros. You will be an assistant to the colonel. I was told you have a talent for computers."

"I guess so."

"You will manage his correspondence, his appointments, his work."

"Why me? I've never done anything like this before. I'm not trained at all."

He ignored my questions. "We understand that the colonel is working with a gang that promotes illegal immigration into Greece through the borders at Evros. We want your help to expose him. Do this, and your criminal record will be expunged. You'll be free to continue your life as if nothing ever happened. Do we have an agreement?"

It didn't take me long to think about it. This was a huge opportunity.

"Who will I be accountable to?"

"Since we don't know who's involved, I'm your only contact. You will receive two months' training. Then, you'll be placed in this position. We have arranged for your transfer to be the assistant colonel. Can we count on you?"

"Do I have a choice?"

"Of course you do. But I need to hear it—a yes or a no."

"Yes," I stated firmly, then we shook hands.

"Your papers are ready. Collect your things. You will come with me now."

Soon after, I found myself in a helicopter. I lost all sense of direction. They delivered me to a military building where I spent two months of intensive training. I learned to handle weapons and did considerable hand-to-hand combat training. I even got a driver's license. It was a hard but useful experience. My trainers were harsh— almost abusive—to the point where I felt like I couldn't take it anymore. I wasn't allowed to communicate with the outside world. They wanted me to be wholly committed to my goal.

But my mind often wandered to thoughts of revenge, thoughts I'd promised to leave behind. I had inner peace as long as I was in contact with my brother. But as soon as we were separated for some time, I was filled with hatred and malice for everything that had happened to me, to us.

After two months, the training had come to an end.

They gave me a story, a fictitious background, and taught me what to say. I was from Athens, and I had just finished high school. I received a military ID. I was an only child, and my parents had a clothing store in the center of Athens. I had gone to public school and was the first of my friends to become a soldier. I didn't have a relationship, but I had a good friend named Natalia, who, at one point, had promised to come see me. She was older than me. We'd met during my summer vacation in Corfu.

They'd given me a photo of my parents for my wallet and one of Natalia's letters saying she missed me. I told this story daily while training.

Then they made me swear a declaration.

"I swear to keep faith in my homeland. Obedience to the constitution, its laws, and resolutions state. Submission to my superiors. To carry out their orders willingly and without contradiction. To defend with faith and devotion, up to the last drop of my blood, the flags. Never give up on them, and never leave them. To act in general as a loyal and ambitious soldier."

They put me on a military plane after that. The rules weren't much different from the reformatory. I had to be accountable for everything. To have my schedule, to do what they told me, whenever they told me, without objection.

Having another name made things difficult for me. I often responded the second time they shouted my new name.

Then, I met Colonel Vellis.

A man in his fifties with black hair, plump eyebrows, and a wrinkled forehead. As a first impression, he didn't look like a man who would engage in illegal activities. But in this world, I had learned to look beyond the image, beyond words, beyond deeds. I knew these people. I could easily spot my peers.

"Well, son, you'll be my right hand from today forward. Whatever happens in this office will stay with us. I'm looking for loyalty. Are you going to be a solid addition to my unit? Or are we both wasting our time?"

He sat behind his desk, both hands spread flat on the desktop.

I stood in my military fatigues as steadily as I could. "Yes, sir."

"That is your office." He pointed to the side. "It will remain clean and free of clutter. There will be consequences if it falls into disarray. Do you understand?"

"Yes, sir."

"Sit down and locate your predecessor's notes. You will need them. Turn on the computer. We have work to do."

"As you command, sir."

I did what he told me without delay. As soon as I was left alone in the office, I placed a bug on his phone as directed by Spyros.

The days passed slowly without any progress. I had conversations with soldiers, and they described the colonel as a calm man without a family. His only life was in the army.

I left the camp one night and explored the border fence with a small flashlight. As bad luck would have it, the dogs detected me and started barking. Reluctantly, I headed back to the camp. I had to be more cautious. Otherwise, I'd be screwed.

On the street, a car approached. I waved the driver down, hoping a ride would get me out of the area before the dogs saw me.

The driver rolled down his window. "Where are you headed?" The driver squinted in the dark at me. "Oh, it's you. What are you doing out here?"

It was the radio operator.

"I need a ride."

"Where should I take you?" he asked as I hopped in the car.

"I had some time off but should be back already."

"What are you doing way out here?"

"I drank too much and lost my way. Since I'm new to the area, getting lost was easy."

"Makes sense," he said as he got the car moving again.

"You?" I asked.

"I live in the north. I was going to see my friends at the border."

"Is that allowed?"

"No," he said, a smile breaking out on his face as he checked his mirrors.

"Oh." I loved acting innocent.

"Can't we break the rules once in a while?"

"Sounds good to me."

"The truth is, I'm familiar with this whole situation. You'll see how things are done around here."

"What do you mean?"

"Nothing, just relax."

To keep him talking, I added, "You may be right. I'll learn in time. Thanks for the ride. I owe you."

"You owe me nothing. Just go inside quickly and don't get yourself punished for wandering from your post."

I exited the car, sure the radio operator knew more than he was saying. I had to keep him close.

In the days that followed, everything went smoothly. I made appointments with Vellis and typed letters and reports. I studied his correspondence carefully and listened to his phone calls, but nothing appeared suspicious. I thought they might have made a mistake in his case until he received a strange phone call.

Vellis gestured for me to leave the office. I obeyed to avoid arousing suspicion. After half an hour, Vellis came looking for me.

"Come back in the office," he ordered.

"Yes, sir."

I figured the phone call was personal. Since I was tracking his calls, I'd learn everything I needed to know in short order.

I took my lunch on my bunk and listened to the short conversation Vellis had when I was ordered out of the office.

"Tomorrow's the day," a deep male-accented voice told Vellis.

"How are we going to do it? I don't want it the same way."

"I've already arranged it."

"What time?"

"Eleven."

"I'll have him there."

Then the line died.

He didn't talk much to me for the rest of the day. Although he loaded me with a lot of work.

Once my job was completed for the day, I hid outside Vellis's house that night. If he left, I would follow him.

The interior lights flickered off after sitting in the dark for an hour. Once Vellis was asleep, I'd find a way in and leave another bug behind.

Twenty minutes later, as I stood to come out of hiding, a vehicle eased up to the house's entrance. A lone woman exited the car.

As she approached the front door, I realized I knew her. It was Angelica. Everyone had good things to say about her, but I didn't expect her to visit Vellis.

I decided to try and take advantage of the opportunity, even though it was a risk. Before she knocked on the door, I was able to slip in behind her. I placed a hand over her mouth. She struggled under my grip, but I tightened my hold, quelling the fight in her. Then I dragged her to the side garden behind a large tree, where I whispered in her ear who I was and that I was saving her. Slowly, I released her, and we faced each other.

"There's nothing to worry about," I said under my breath.

She nodded, then turned away and shouted for help.

I clamped a hand over her mouth and grabbed my knife.

"If you do that again," I whispered, the tip of the blade against her cheek, "you'll leave this place with a scar on your face."

She nodded enthusiastically this time.

I waited an extra moment, then took my hand away again.

"When you go inside, I need you to take him outside for five minutes, but leave the balcony door open."

"And why would I do that?" she asked, disdain evident in her tone.

"Just do it. The less you know, the better."

"And if I don't?"

"Don't fuck with me. What Vellis is into is serious, way above our heads. Just do what I tell you so you stay clean. I don't want this to get bloody."

I sensed her trembling. I had scared her.

She nodded in the affirmative, and I released her. She went to Vellis's front door and rang the bell. Almost immediately, Vellis opened it, wearing a robe.

I moved stealthily to the other side of the house, where the balcony was. I carefully climbed the porch and, with my back on the wall, approached the glass doors.

"Honey." I was close enough to hear Angelica's voice through the closed door. "I'll open the door to have some fresh air."

"Don't bother with the door. Come closer to me."

There was a pause, then, "I forgot something in the car."

"Come here, I said. I'm not paying you to be late."

"Sweetheart, I forgot to bring a toy. Come with me, then. You won't regret it."

Her tone was playful, so playful that I felt disgusted. That's what Kiki would have said to her customers.

As soon as they stepped outside the front of the house, I slipped into the back and searched for the phone. I left the bedroom, climbed the stairs, and entered his office. Once the small device was planted inside Vellis's phone, I searched the papers on his desk. One document caught my attention. It had a phone number and the name Takis. I took a photo of it and moved to the office door. At the top of the stairs, I heard voices.

They had returned.

"Are you kidding me?" Vellis shouted. "Who do you think you are?"

Something hit the floor hard. I assumed that was Angelica being knocked down.

"I swear to you," she pleaded. "I thought I'd brought it with me." She was crying now.

She crawled into view at the bottom of the stairs. Vellis stood over her in a threatening manner.

"What you do for the other soldiers doesn't work for me. Do you understand? I am the colonel, and you will do what I tell you to do."

"Yes, sweetheart, whatever you want." Angelica tried to get to her feet.

Vellis pushed her down again, grabbed her by the hair, and dragged her toward the bedroom while she screamed a high-pitched wail. She scrambled on the floor behind him, trying to lessen the pressure on her scalp while keeping up.

A moment later, the bedroom door slammed shut behind them.

I vibrated with my feelings of hatred and revenge, my fist clenching and unclenching. Hearing her scream and knowing I couldn't save her drove me mad.

I left Vellis's home resolved to kill the man.

After the mission, I would kill him. Of this, I had no doubt.

Since no one was around to judge him, I had done it. His sentence was death.

As I strode away, I wondered if there was something I could do, then snapped my fingers at the idea that came to me.

I took a stone, threw it at Vellis's front window, and ran from the area as glass shattered behind me.

After a few days of not seeing Angelica, I heard she'd visited her mother. That either meant she was in the hospital or she'd disappeared.

The colonel had come to his office the next day as if nothing had happened the previous night. He dictated normal tasks for me throughout the day.

I'd been trying to get in touch with Spyros for several days, but I couldn't find him anywhere. I left him messages but still hadn't heard from him. This worried me.

I had recorded Vellis's conversations and put them in an envelope. I wanted to mail the envelope to Spyros, but I wrote my brother's school address instead.

Someone had to have a file of what was going on up here.

Someone knocked on the outer door. I got up from my desk to answer it.

Spyros stood there in full uniform.

"Nikos," he stated in a firm tone.

"Yes, sir." I saluted him.

"I came to see what you're doing."

"Lieutenant?"

"Are things going smoothly?"

"Yes, sir. The colonel has gone to supervise some work."

"I want a full report of what you know up to date."

"I've been looking for you for several days now, sir. I've left many messages. Do we have any assistance?"

"What do you mean?"

"Today, something will take place. They called him yesterday. He needs surveillance. I can't do it alone."

"Do you have recordings?"

I nodded. "His conversation yesterday and one from today. But I didn't have time to listen to today's yet."

"Well done, soldier. Give me what you've got, and I'll watch him from here."

"But …?"

"Leave it to me. You did what you had to do. You're relieved of duty at the end of the day. Don't come tomorrow. You'll fly to Athens tomorrow, and you will be a free man in a few days. Start dreaming, soldier."

The rest of the day slipped by in an agitated blur. I didn't have confirmation that Vellis would have the punishment he deserved.

At the end of my shift, I listened to the conversations I'd recorded. Vellis spoke of a meeting near the river, close to the abandoned outpost, at twenty-three hundred hours that night.

There were only a few outposts in that area, but I didn't know which one Vellis was referring to. I had heard rumors inside the camp about how Turks helped immigrants cross the border for one million drachmas per head. They preferred to bring them by boat and leave them on the shore. Then, the immigrants found the nearest villages and surrendered to the authorities. After that, they were sent to detention centers. Most declared themselves citizens of a country at war in order to seek asylum.

I didn't understand what Vellis was involved in, and there was no way I would leave without knowing.

By nine-thirty that night, I was outside his house. I had a flashlight and a knife—I didn't need anything else. I expected he'd make his move tonight. I didn't have any sort of plan, only a target.

This would be his last night on earth.

After several hours of waiting, a car approached then parked outside Vellis's home. The car door opened, and a tall male figure got out. I wasn't close enough to be able to recognize him. The man knocked on Vellis's front door and waited. After a few moments, Vellis exited his house, and they both got in the car. I followed as best I could on a bike I'd snatched from the village. The roads were bad, and the river closed. I had to be extra careful as I couldn't afford to lose him.

Twenty minutes later, I hid behind bushes, watching Vellis and his companion. They were waiting for a boat. They had lit cigarettes while talking. Due to the quiet calm of the area, I could easily hear what they were saying.

"It's too late."

"You're right. They should already be here."

"Did you get rid of the other one?"

"That won't be a problem. He'll go home tomorrow."

"Did you convince him?"

"I don't think that matters. What he wanted from the beginning was his freedom."

"I can't wait for him to leave. He's exhausting to be around like I had a predator nearby. Sometimes, he got a dark look in his eyes that made me shudder. I don't understand why you chose him."

The man faced Vellis, blowing smoke at him. "Are you an idiot? They were onto you. Didn't we advise you to remain low-key? I had to give them something, and he was a perfect choice. A nobody—he means nothing."

"Still, he took the job quite seriously."

The other man dropped his cigarette and stomped it out with his boot. "He's a lowlife, a nobody. I snatched him from a reformatory and dangled the carrot of an expunged record and freedom in front of him. If he fucked with us, his credibility was shot. If he succeeded in any way, he was only reporting to me. This was a perfect plan, through and through."

After a moment, Vellis asked, "Why am I here? What does the Turk want with me?"

"Probably to ask you about the papers."

"Didn't you tell him it was too dangerous?"

"Doesn't matter. He wants an up-close meeting."

"What did you do with the money?"

"I arranged it as we discussed."

"Tell it to me in detail while we wait."

"I got one million per head, plus another million for their documents. I put it all in the box."

They fell silent.

I understood everything now. Spyros was also part of the plan. I was only there to show he was doing a good job. I was used. I was nothing.

Although, I didn't mind that. I wasn't interested in justice in the army, the immigrants, or their traffickers. That wasn't my fight.

I was only interested in vengeance. Men like Vellis hurt Kiki. Someone had to pay.

So, let it be Vellis.

Finally, the boat arrived, and they dragged it up onto the shore.

The idiots had left their car unlocked. I slipped into the back seat and waited, only lifting my head a few times to peer out the windows.

They all carried flashlights, and I could make out their faces at times. The guy who had offered me a ride the other night was with a Turk—no great surprise. Next to him stood fifteen troubled, darker people.

Along with the smell of the river, I could smell their hope, despair, fear, and redemption. They thought that when they got here, their suffering would end. What they couldn't know was that their troubles were just beginning for some of them.

After a short conversation by the river's shore, most of which I couldn't hear, they headed toward the car. I sat quietly in the back seat, hoping the radio guy wouldn't come along, too.

I wasn't so lucky. As they approached, my heart pounded hard as I considered a course of action. I squeezed the knife in my hands to quell their slight tremble.

Before reaching the car, the Turk turned and shouted something at everyone, then drew a weapon. Everyone raised their hands, including Vellis and Spyros. The immigrants cowered in fear by the shore.

Spyros spoke to him in Turkish, but the man seemed agitated about something, gesturing with his hands for Spyros to be silent. Someone distracted the Turk, and then Spyros drew his weapon and fired.

As the Turk fell to his knees, he fired back, hitting Spyros.

Vellis ran toward the car to save his own ass. An immigrant ran behind Vellis and grabbed him about the waist. They dropped to the ground and fought like wild animals, arms flailing, legs kicking.

Vellis was much stronger, though. He threw punch after punch into the immigrant's stomach and face. Even after the man had lost consciousness, Vellis kept up his assault, smashing his face until Vellis was covered in blood.

Drunk with anger and adrenaline, Vellis entered the car and started the engine. I stayed in the back seat and waited for my chance.

With so many shots fired, it was only a matter of time before the soldiers guarding the tower would find us. I heard Vellis's gasping and sensed his anxiety, but I remained patient for my turn.

When I was certain we were clear of the area, I eased up in the seat and placed the knife at his throat. Vellis jerked in the seat.

"What do you want?" he asked. "Money? I have plenty. I'll give it to you."

"Stop the car."

"Where? Here? It's just fields."

"Stop now," I shouted. "And leave the engine running."

Like a frightened mouse, he listened to my orders.

With the knife in one hand, I opened my door and stepped from the vehicle.

"Get out," I said.

He shoved his door open so abruptly that it bumped into me, knocking me over.

He scrambled to get back in and leave. I pivoted on the ground, grabbed his leg with my free hand, and then stabbed the knife with the other.

Vellis's scream echoed throughout the surrounding fields, but no one was close enough to hear him.

He dropped to the ground, unable to support himself on his wounded leg. I grabbed him by his neck while he struggled to free himself. I'd subdued him, my arm around his neck, his fingers clawing at my forearm.

Then, I detected a whisper as he tried to say something.

I released his neck enough to make out the word.

"Why?" he cried.

Like a punch to the gut, that word hit me full force. Was it possible Vellis didn't know why? After all the harm he'd done and was still doing, how could he not know why?

My arm had relaxed, my hands loosened. At that moment, he snatched at my knife, secured it, and stabbed me in the abdomen.

The pain hadn't hit me yet, though I knew it was coming. So I fought him with everything I had, punching at his nose and throat until Vellis stopped moving.

My revenge was defeated, my target dead. I lie on the ground, covered in blood, panting with pain now.

I wiped down the knife, clearing it of my prints. Then I took the stone and hit my own head enough to break the skin. It hurt like hell, but I had to do it. With blood streaming down my face, I got in the car and drove down the road until I fainted behind the steering wheel due to blood loss.

When I opened my eyes again, I was in a hospital. Several military officers surrounded me in short order, waiting for some kind of statement.

"Finally," one of the officers said. I'd never seen him before. "We'll get the answers we need. Son, are you feeling okay to talk?"

"Probably," I said, looking for a doctor. I tried to sit up, but the pain in my stomach was too intense. The bastard Vellis had left his mark on me. Also, I felt like my head was going to split in two.

"Tell us everything you know," the officer said.

"I don't remember a thing," I whispered. "Everything's blurry."

The doctor rushed into the room and leaned close to examine my pupils.

"Let him rest," he said. "It's quite common to have a partial lack of memory after a blow to the head or a traumatic event. It should all come back to you soon."

The officers in the room eased back from my bedside, displeasure on their faces.

"I'm sorry I can't help you at this time," I said, innocence lacing my tone.

This would give me time to learn what happened to the others and build a more convincing story. I had no intention of going to prison again. Once was enough. I didn't need a second.

After leaving my room, they placed security outside my door. They were suspicious of something. I could see it in their eyes, and I knew they wouldn't let me go that easily.

After a while, a nurse came to change the bandage on the head. She was tall, with beautiful, sweet eyes and a glowing face. She seemed to truly care about her patients. With great care, she began the arduous task of removing my bandage.

"How do you feel?" she asked.

"Physically, not so bad. I'm more worried about the others."

"I am not allowed to discuss what happened with you," she said, glancing over her shoulder at the security officers watching from outside the room.

"Please, what happened to me? How did I get these injuries? If someone gave me something to think about, perhaps it would shed some light on the darkness that's my current memory."

She glanced back at the door again, then stared into my eyes. "They're all dead," she muttered, only loud enough for me to hear her.

She wouldn't say another word.

After she finished with the bandage, she left me alone.

If they were all dead, I could spin the story any way I wanted. After a day of isolation, I told the soldiers I remembered something. Shortly after that, they took my statement.

I spoke of Vellis bringing immigrants across the borders and how he gave them counterfeit papers for a hefty fee. I explained that my purpose was to expose him. During a meeting with his Turkish counterpart, he took me with him and told me to wait in the car's back seat. While he negotiated the payment, a fight broke out with the Turk, who shot at the others. I couldn't see their faces because it was too dark. Then, after letting the immigrants go, the Turk took Vellis as a hostage and got in the car. I stayed hidden in the back seat until I tried to disarm him. Vellis stopped the car and spilled out into the ditch, fighting in a field. The Turk took a stone and hit me on the head. I lost consciousness, and when I woke up again, I saw Vellis injured. I tried my best to help him but knew I needed to drive for help. I think I lost consciousness behind the wheel and woke up here.

"Can you describe the Turk?"

"I was mostly hidden in the car's back seat. It was too dark."

"Is there anything else you can tell us?"

I should've been awarded an Oscar for my performance.

"We caught some of the illegal immigrants," a short man with a mustache and round glasses said. "But they're keeping their mouths shut. They're terrified."

"I don't think I have anything else to say."

They left my hospital room disappointed.

I had covered my tracks well. There were no eyewitnesses, and I had no motive. There were no fingerprints, and the Turk had murdered Vellis, which was something no one could ever corroborate.

It was perfect. No one knew a thing, and the immigrants, if they ever spoke, wouldn't contradict my story since they'd never even seen me.

Upon investigating me further, they'd learn that I was trained to become Vellis's assistant for two months to expose him. I was one of the good ones.

The next day, my guards were relieved of duty. It seemed the danger had disappeared.

When I woke hours later, I had a visitor.

"Kostas?"

"What happened, beast? How'd you do it?" He hugged me before I could answer.

I was so happy to see him. I felt like I was taking a fresh breath.

"Did you hear what happened?"

"Yes." Kostas nodded. "I was informed yesterday. I took the first plane out here. I need to believe you're telling the absolute truth, and I haven't unnecessarily risked my neck and career." He pierced me with his stare. That full-of-suspicion glare he'd used before—the same look he gave me after Kiki's death.

I cleared my throat. "I swear to you. I told them the truth. That was how things went down. I've not hidden a thing. Why would I? There's no reason."

"They will let you go, but only under my surveillance. Consider yourself lucky I have solid connections. Otherwise, I don't know how you would get out of here."

"So, it's over? I'm done?" I remember saying it with relief. By solid connections, he meant he knew who to bribe and who to pay off.

"Yes, brother, finally." He spoke with a wide smile. My loving brother, my good version, my good soul. "You can make a fresh start now. I have some money, so maybe you can stay somewhere until I finish school, and then we can stay together."

I felt his warmth in my heart. "That would be perfect. I can finally be happy."

"But before you get happy, I have something to give you." He took out a pink notebook from the inside pocket of his uniform.

"What's this?"

"I thought you'd want to read something. A policeman helped me get this. I found it in Kiki's police files as proof of a crime."

"What crime?"

"The assassination of Stratos Diamantidis."

"Oh ..."

"Our father," he said in a calm voice.

I stared at him in bewilderment. My mind seemed to have stopped. I couldn't think of anything. I was empty.

Time seemed to freeze as I took the pink notebook, which had hand drawings of little flowers on its outside. It looked like a little girl's diary —nothing to do with murder.

I didn't know whether I should look at it or not. I wasn't sure if I should learn what happened or if I even wanted to.

Who was Kiki's accomplice in our abandonment at that hospital all those years ago?

Who was my father?

Did he know we existed? Or did he die before he learned about his sons?

I held the notebook close, knowing this would be a darker road than I'd previously traveled.

Chapter 11

March 3rd

March 3RD

My dear Diary, today is the first day I hold you in my hands. Since I don't have a close girlfriend, and my parents don't understand me, I will share my thoughts with you. Here at home, things are bad. My father is always away at work, and when he comes home, he's on edge and lashes out at me and Mom. Sometimes, when he drinks too much, he beats us both. Mom told me not to pay any attention to him because he was tired and brought home our food. We must always respect and serve the man who brings food to our home.

I know I'm still young, only twelve years old, but when I grow up, I'll become someone who can make a difference in this world. That's what I believe, even if Dad tells me I was born to serve and not dream.

"You can't eat letters. There's no need for you to study. Just learn how to treat your husband, and you'll be fine." He tells me this stuff every day. Only Mom understands me and secretly believes in me. She tells me that I must read and study to not become like her, and I shouldn't *need* anyone.

December 6th

It's been four years since I first took you in my arms. I couldn't write my thoughts then. The first day, I fought with my mom, and she took you from my arms and hid you. I wonder why she didn't tear you apart. Now I found you, and I wish I never had. As I was gathering her clothes, there you were. She had hidden you under Grandma's jewelry. Now, the jewels are mine. What should I do with them? Nothing matters anymore. Maybe I shouldn't live. But how would I do it? I can't survive without her. He is like a ghost hovering inside the house. I can tell he exists just because wherever he goes, he leaves behind the scent of beer. He told me it was a big accident. Even the police confirm this. But I don't think so. He may not have done it with his own hands, but it works out to be the same for me.

One day, he will pay. I hate him and don't know how I stay in the same house with him. But I'm scared. I have no money, and I haven't finished school. I have no other home and no light in my life. I wish I had her near me to smile at me once more, to hug me and cover me with blankets to sleep. Give me a sweet goodnight kiss on the forehead. I would never scream at her again, I would always help her, and I wouldn't let him touch her again. I can't write anymore. I can't stand the pain and the sadness, it's a lot ... I can't stand it ...

September 15th

I had decided to never write again. These few lines I've written so far only bring me sadness and nothing else. But something has changed. I met a man, looked him in the eye, and knew. A tall, thin brunette with black eyes and a playful look. He came today from another school. He is so handsome that my heart fluttered for the first time. I've liked boys before, but nothing compares to this. I heard his name today. Stratos.

September 16th

I am absolutely happy. Stratos was officially introduced today He came and sat next to me at recess. I learned a few things about him. He's older than me. His parents had stayed abroad for a while, and he missed school years. So he's two years older than me. Ideal difference. He makes funny jokes and makes me laugh. God, how much I missed smiling to bury a little of my soul's darkness. My life is finally making sense.

October 1st

Every day I look anxiously to see if he's come. He has three days to show up. Is he sick? Maybe he changed to a different school? Did he leave? Nobody has news of him. How can I be so unlucky? I felt joy inside of me after so long.

I didn't pay attention to my father's voice. I just didn't care and waited for the next day. I'm so tired of being the woman of the house, though. I have to do everything by myself, and the only thing he does is work, eat, drink, and sleep. I want to live. I can no longer deal with this grief daily like an insidious poison that destroys me. I must leave. Stratos was my only joy. He was the only one who seemed to care about me and didn't feel sorry for me like the rest. He wasn't afraid to see my darkness like the others. I'm tired of being in isolation because of my father. He never let me invite people home or gave me pocket money to go out. I'm never allowed to go to a party. He's afraid bad influences will destroy my mental health. I must be "pure" to find a good husband and marry. I wonder how he still lets me go to school and doesn't lock me in our home. Is it a real home, though?

I wish I had money to disappear from this neighborhood that I have hated so much. Every time my mother's screams could be heard, they closed their shutters not to hear her. You see, people mustn't intervene in our family. When misery overwhelms a family, the neighbors isolate them like they're afraid that the suffering will touch them, and they don't want to be infected. Nobody intervenes as if it's a contagious disease. This makes them all accomplices in the silence. All accomplices.

December 22nd

Today, I am very happy. Finally, I feel my heart beating again. He was waiting for me after the school Christmas celebration. He was outside the door holding a rose. As soon as I saw him, I felt a burning on the inside. I must have turned red, but I didn't care. He gave me the rose and then a kiss on the cheek. He hadn't forgotten my birthday. We took a bus and went down to the center of Athens for a walk. While we were walking, he made me laugh. He didn't want to discuss why he had disappeared and always changed the subject. He took my hand, and then he hugged me. My heart pounded so hard I wondered if he'd feel it. I wanted him to kiss me. I was dying for him to kiss me.

Nevertheless, he didn't. It doesn't matter, though, as long as I'm with him. I could smell his clothes. I could feel his body on mine. The tighter he hugged me, the more I wanted to surrender to him. I wasn't interested in anything else. I would do it if he told me to run away with him. I asked him when I would see him again, and he said he'd find me. Will he find me, or will he disappear again?

January 3rd

I still don't have any news about him. Why is he doing this to me? Why is he torturing me? Where is he? I can't stand the anticipation anymore. I'm unhappy, and I'm crying. Every time I listen to ballads, I can't restrain myself. Fortunately, my father doesn't see me at all, so I don't have to give him explanations.

January 4th

Today, I went to the bakery, and he found me. He drove a motorbike, and I sat on the back, hugging him. I've missed him so much. There's no doubt I live and breathe only for him. He said he wanted to show me something. We found ourselves on a hill with an incredible view. He kissed me, and it was full of fire. I had never kissed a boy before. I felt my heart beating so fast and loud that I wondered if it would be damaged. Then he stroked my hair and held me even tighter. I wish that moment never ended. I was so happy.

He came to my house at night. My father was sleeping. He threw stones at my window to get my attention as he wanted to tell me something. I snuck outside. Then he told me something that made me sick to my stomach. He confessed he had a girlfriend. He'd been in a relationship for two years. He didn't expect to feel the way he did about me, but he couldn't separate from Isabella. I felt my world fall apart. I didn't want to hear anything else. I ran away and came immediately to write it, sobbing so I wouldn't wake my father and have more trouble. I can't stand it. It's too much for me. Why did he do that to me?

January 5th

He found me on the street again, but I didn't want to talk to him. He was walking with me, trying to make me feel better. I explained that to have any relationship with him, he had to break up with his girlfriend. I can't share him, and I can't bear the thought of him being with another girl. Stratos then took my hand and led me to an apartment building. We got on an elevator, where he hugged and violently kissed me. I tried to push him away, but it was so hard. I couldn't resist him. I want him only for myself. I want him to love me and only me. Break up with that bitch and be with me. Forever with me.

January 6th

Today, all the shops are closed. I don't have an excuse to go out, and my father is inside. I can't stand it, and I want to see Stratos. I can't help not seeing him, even if it's just one day, to smell his scent, linger in his warm embrace, see his smile, and laugh at his jokes. I can't. Stand. It.

January 7th

Schools opened today. He occluded my thoughts—he was all I could think about. Teachers shouted at me because I wasn't paying attention. I stared at the clock, waiting for the day to pass. After school, he was waiting for me on his motorbike. We took a long ride. I was so happy. He took me to a forest where we were alone. He rolled on top of me and kissed me furiously. Within minutes, he had me undressed on the cold grass. He touched me everywhere. I couldn't resist. I'm so in love with him and kept telling him so. He whispered in my ear how much he wanted me. It was my first time. I am full of love and affection. It doesn't matter where he is. He'll break up with her at some point. He promised me.

January 15th

I haven't seen him for days. Could he have only wanted sex? I can't even stand the thought. A friend of his came to see me today, Mario. He accompanied me home. I don't know why. Of course, I didn't tell him anything about Stratos and me. He asked for my phone number, but I didn't give it to him. If my father were ever to pick up a call?

Stratos came to my house tonight, throwing stones at my window again. I went down the stairs, quiet as a cat. I wanted to swear at him. I was so angry he'd disappeared. But he hugged me and took me to the back part of my house. He undressed me within seconds, and we made love on the terrace table. Then he left as fast as he'd come. I was lost.

January 16th

I don't know what to think, what to guess. Mario asked me out. Officially. I didn't know what to tell him. I didn't expect to have so much interest from boys. It was all so sudden. Nobody ever looked at me. Anyway, I accepted. I don't know why, but I agreed. The truth is, I was flattered. I had an English class, but I skipped it. We had an hour and a half, so he took me on his motorbike and sat in a playground. There, he told me that Stratos urged him to meet me because I was a good girl and we would have a good time together. I've never heard this kind of bullshit. How is it possible to be together, make love with so much passion, and then urge his friend to come onto me? I am full of questions and flooded with anger now. How can he do that? How can he want to share me?

I didn't show any of these emotions to Mario. He bent down and kissed me tenderly and with affection. I didn't react. It was just a kiss. What would be the harm in that? If he wants me to be with someone else and he can stand it, I will do it, but I won't see him again. I don't want to see him again. He can be with his Isabella forever and cheat on her every day. They deserve to be together.

Mario accompanied me to the English class, holding my hand. He was so affectionate and kind. He wasn't bad at all. Blond with blue eyes and a nice voice. Maybe I should leave Stratos behind and move on with Mario.

January 19th

Today, I learned news that shook me. Stratos had an accident on his motorcycle, and Mario told me to go to his house and check if he was okay. I couldn't believe my ears. I lost my mind. Of course, I didn't want to show anything. I went to his house for the first time. He lived in a poor house. I didn't expect him to be there. He had given me the impression that he had enough money for himself and his family.

Mario took me to his room. That's where I saw her. He was hugging her. A girl, a little younger than me, thin, with big eyes and curly hair. For a second, I was shaken, but I hid it well. He didn't expect to see me there but didn't hesitate to pull his hands away from her. He was slightly injured. I shouldn't worry. We spoke as if we had known each other for a long time. What irony. Isabella left, and the three of us stayed. Stratos sent Mario to bring him water, and then we were alone. He told me to come at night to talk. I wanted to resist, but I didn't. I couldn't believe his nerve. Mario brought him the water, and the discussion stopped. Then we left.

Luckily, my father had taken over a building that was quite some distance from our house, and he would be away for the whole weekend. I was free to do whatever I wanted. Mario came to my house at eight. He sat on the couch and hugged me. He told me that I was unique, and he wanted to have a relationship with me. Then he undressed me. I wanted to resist, but I didn't. I felt like I was punishing Stratos somehow. I didn't hurt anyone, so no one cared. Mario would never learn any of it.

When Mario left, I bathed and got ready to visit Stratos. I had to find him, hit him, and make him leave me alone to continue my life. When I arrived at Stratos's home, I slowly opened the door. He'd left it open so no one would know I was there. I went to his room, where he was waiting for me. As soon as I entered, he hugged me and kissed me passionately. I tried to push him away, but he grabbed my hands.

I cursed him, but he closed my mouth with kisses full of passion. I'm weak, so weak when I'm near him. We made love once again. I should have felt guilty as I slept with two different men that night, but I don't feel it. Stratos told me we must have a good time, and that's all that matters. Maybe he's right.

Since we want each other so much, why not just have a good time? Since my heart desires him desperately, why shouldn't I do everything I can to be with him?

February 10th

I broke up with Mario. I told him I wasn't ready for a relationship, which was the absolute truth. He didn't seem to care that much. I didn't want to cheat on him. He treated me so well. In the meantime, Stratos had introduced me to another friend of his, who was really lovely. He also had a big motorbike and took me on great rides. But in the end, I couldn't be with him either. It's a lot of confusion and a lot of lies. I have to move on with my life. I need to talk to Stratos and tell him to stop chasing me. I wish I weren't so weak in front of him and so addicted. I keep doing what he tells me, as he tells me, without being able to react or understand why.

We had an appointment at night. I had to sneak out again. I had found the trick. I left through the window as soon as he drank his beers and slept heavily. My father never knew. So, I did it today as well. He was waiting for me at the playground. When he saw me, he hugged me and kissed me. He said he found a way to raise money so we could be together as long as I trusted him, which was easy for me. We inhaled some powder. He said it was not terrible, nor was it addictive. All that would happen was that we would have a good time.

I felt great joy, indescribable joy, and a slight dizziness. He undressed me. I couldn't resist. After a few minutes, a stranger came to the playground. He told me not to be afraid and laid me down. As he was kissing me, another one came and kissed me, too. I couldn't react for some reason. I couldn't resist.

I don't remember what happened next. I woke up, and all I can recall was Stratos showing me a lot of money. It's so funny because I was about to break up with him. What happened yesterday? Did I have sex with other men? How could I? I don't remember anything. I need to see him again soon. I need answers.

February 11th

I went where we met yesterday to see if he would be there. I waited for a while, and then he came, too. When he saw me, his face brightened, and he tried to kiss me, but I pulled away. He showed me his wallet. Inside, it had five thousand drachmas. He told me that I'd made the money by sleeping with the other guy and that this was how to run away together. Then he hugged me and kissed my neck. I pulled away again, and it angered him. He explained that if we ran away together, we could be together forever, and if I didn't do as he told me, it would show that I didn't want him.

I said there must be another way. He said there was no other way. If I want him, we need to raise money. That was it. Sleep with ten men, leave together, and then we'll be happy. He said he had even found the perfect place. Then he would get a job, and we would stay together forever as long as I made this one small sacrifice. He said he would look after me. No one would treat me wrong as he wouldn't allow it. He told me how much it hurt him that I had to sacrifice like this and sleep with other men, but he'd do it for our love. He'd endure anything for me. I wonder if this is real love.

February 13th

Yesterday, I made the second appointment. He gave me the powder so I'd be calmer. Fortunately, we went to his house, and it wasn't in public like the other time. I felt so uncomfortable and didn't like it. I felt dirty and wanted to cry. But I'm trying for his sake. I'm patient. At some point, this will end, and I will get closer and closer to the dream. I close my eyes and think about the life that awaits me. I want this so much. I'm with him. And now we have another five thousand drachmas. Nine left.

February 14th

Today is Valentine's Day. I'm anxious to see what he'll do I want so much to spend a romantic night together. To walk, hug, whisper to each other, and hold hands. I'm in love. I can't believe it.

February 15th

Nothing went as I expected. I arrived full of expectations. I was looking forward to seeing him. He came to me holding a flower. He told me that we couldn't spend time together. He had someone who gave him ten thousand drachmas for two hours with me. He could not refuse as it was a lot of money. He told me that he's an important man and I should please him. I didn't like that at all. He took me to a cheap motel, a room that smelled of moisture. I got undressed and went under the covers. He took a scarf, and he covered my eyes. He told me to remain blindfolded throughout the ordeal as I'm not supposed to know who the man is. That scared me, but here I was, and I couldn't back off. The man came, whoever he was, and he fell on me in a rage. I did what he asked me to do, but it was too much violence. I protested some, and the man enjoyed it more. I hated myself for it. As soon as he left, Stratos came, and he took off my scarf. I cried, and he hugged me, and we stayed that way for quite some time. He told me that he loved me and thanked me for the sacrifice. We're almost free, he said. Seven more to go.

February 20th

After that night, I had no news of him, which worried me. I went to our place, but he was nowhere. Was he tired of waiting? Did he return to his Isabella? I can't even think of it. I can't imagine he'd do that after what I'd done for him. Would he turn his back on me? There's a deep sadness in my soul. I'm so lonely without him. No man has loved me so much, not even my father. He made me feel like someone cared about me and I was not just a maid and a fool schoolgirl. I wish my mother were here. We had our issues, but at least I felt someone existed for me. It would have been different if I hadn't been banned from having girlfriends. Now I'm alone, so alone …

March 10th

He finally showed up. I thought it was all over. Yesterday, he came and picked me up from school. We went for a short walk. He had many things to arrange. He told me he was looking for a place to stay, but we needed more money than he expected. He told me we couldn't be together like that. I don't understand why we can't, though. We needed more money, I guess. He promised that we would get married later. He had never said such a thing. I'm so happy. But first, we had to solve the money problem. He will work as a waiter on weekends, and I will make a few visits, and everything will be fine. I can leave my asshole father and live as I want without one oppressing me—and without school. If I have Stratos, I don't need anything else. I will find something to do, too. Then we will make our own family, and finally, everything will be wonderful in my life. I will not go to school, so I'm available for more male customers. We will collect the money so much faster this way. I just have to be patient.

March 17th

Now that I'm not attending school, I have much time to make money. Stratos arranged seven appointments for me, one per day. But because they were his friends, he had to lower the price because they didn't have much money. So everyone gave one thousand drachmas. Fortunately, no one bothered me. They had a good time, and I did everything they asked. They were happy. I was told they would arrange a visit again. I vomited after every time. I hate them and myself. As Stratos says, however, the purpose sanctifies the means. I'm not really sure what that means, but I'm going with it.

March 25th

Today is a holiday. My father is home, too. I feel like a beast in a cage. We don't talk to each other. We have nothing to say. Everyone is in their own world. I did all the work around the house. I cooked and locked myself here in my room. As I was cleaning my dad's closets, I found a gun. It had to be up there for a long time. I will keep it in my closet. If a thief comes, Dad is likelier to shoot himself than the thief.

March 26th

I had another appointment with that mystery man. I didn't want to as I was afraid of him. Stratos gave me the powder and sent me inside blindfolded. Whatever he did to me, I didn't complain. I locked the house of my dreams in my mind. My new home would have a garden, lots of flowers, and a dog. After he was done, my entire body hurt, but ten thousand drachmas were ours. I earned every one of them.

April 15th

I take drugs every time before each appointment. It has become necessary. I'm afraid that the money I'm making is going to drugs. If I'm a few hours late to have them, I go crazy. Then I find Stratos, and he gives me the drugs. I feel great after, and I can go to all my appointments. He told me that I was close to finishing everything. To collect more money, I had a morning with multiple appointments. I went to a hotel room and fucked with more than ten men. This time, even though I was on drugs, it was unbearable. Their breath smelled of alcohol. They were unwashed and dirty. I don't know where he found them, but I can't take it anymore. I want to stop.

April 16th

He told me he had another appointment, and then that was it. If I didn't go, he wouldn't give me drugs. Dead end.

April 17th

I'm crying as I write these words to you. I accidentally pulled off my scarf and saw his face. The old man was shocked because I knew him and he knew me. I'm locked in my room and won't let him in. In so many sexual visits, he was fucking his own daughter. I was satisfying my father's abnormal desires without him knowing it, without me knowing it. He preferred underage girls. Disgusting. But Stratos? He knew. I was beaten as never before. Before my father knew it was me, he called me a whore and punched me repeatedly. My face was swollen, and Stratos wasn't there to help me.

I crawled home through my unbearable pain. I want to hide from the world and let no one see me. Now that I'm writing, he's banging on the door and cursing my name. He's so drunk. I'm afraid that he'll hit me again. I will take his gun with me and run out the window. I'm terrified. I have no idea what he'll do to me. The best thing is if I was dead. I don't deserve anything more. I disappointed him. I disappointed myself.

Maybe I was born to be a whore, using drugs. It would be better if I died right now, escaping this nightmare. Maybe if I went to Stratos, things would change. There's no way he could've known he was my father. He would never do that to me. I will pack and find him to put an end to this. I will leave you here. Let my father find you. To understand how non-existent he was in my life. To understand that he never gave me paternal affection and never gave me love. He was always indifferent whether I lived or died. All he needed was a cleaner, a cook, not a daughter. Goodbye, Father. End diary.

"What happened next?" I asked.

Kostas glanced at the floor. "Kiki went to find Stratos at his house. She was full of hope for a new beginning. She found him with another girl, and she couldn't take it. She shot him. Then she went to prison while she was already pregnant."

"By whom?"

Kostas looked up and met my gaze. "She said Stratos was our father, but no one could tell."

"I don't know how to react to all this."

"You can forgive her, for starters," he said, touching me on the shoulder.

I didn't respond. I was shocked by this whole story. It's so easy to blame Kiki for everything, but I finally understood she was also a victim of family paranoia and abandonment. She got involved with the wrong person and paid for it for the rest of her life.

There was no one for her, no one.

I need to tell someone, my friend, before they kill me.

I forgive her.

Kiki, my mom, forgive me ... please ...

Chapter 12

It has been a long time since then, many years. I stayed with my brother while trying to find a job. I worked hard to leave my past behind. However, there were two things that I couldn't let go of. My mother's story and the bitch that put me in the reformatory. I'm making a great effort not to hurt her. Sometimes, I think that if I don't take revenge on her, my soul will never rest. It isn't that I just want to kill her—I want to make her suffer. Then my brother comes to my mind, and I calm down.

He graduated from police school and decided to go to special police forces. I had some jobs, but I was bored and quit. I couldn't be happy with anything. The thing is, now that I think about it more, I need to be the boss. It's challenging for me to obey assholes. I wanted something else. I didn't know what it was, but I knew it wasn't food delivery, souvlaki wrapper, driver, storekeeper, or any of those kinds of occupation. But I did it for Kostas and to stay away from trouble.

For the first few days, he told me how different his training was. I didn't know what these guys were doing, so I stared at him like an idiot when he told me that their mission was to handle exceptionally dangerous situations such as terrorist acts, abductions, hostage rescue, dangerous criminal arrests, dealing with fortified persons, protection of high-risk individuals, and a host of other things that I can't remember. I wondered how he came out like that. Sometimes, I teased him and called him a masked superhero, a punisher of crime.

He was so excited about his police equipment, as if he was a small child and was given sweets. A bulletproof vest, ballistic helmet with visor, gas mask, tactical uniform, and a bunch of weapons that I didn't even know they existed. A Glock, Sig Sauer, revolvers, submachine guns, rifles, machine guns, and shotguns.

As I listened, I thought about how much money I would make if I stole from their warehouses. But no, I wouldn't do that to him. I love him too much to embarrass him. If it weren't for him, I would be rotting somewhere in prison. He proudly told me he was only one of one hundred and fifty men who made it and how hard it was to get in. He didn't have many incidents to intervene—all he did was train. Of course, that didn't hurt him. He wanted to be the first, the bravest, the toughest.

To me, he was just a big brother. He took care of me, fed me when I didn't have a job, and cheered me up. Although, I couldn't bear to hang out with his friends. I didn't belong there.

Sometimes, I felt like I was making fun of him. I know deep inside me, there's only darkness. I focus so hard on keeping the bad shit hidden, but I never know how much leaks out when I'm tired and not paying attention.

I remember when they gave him a wireless radio. He listened to police frequencies all night long like he was going to put on his cloak and go punish the criminals of Athens. He listened in the hope that the time would come when he would intervene in a crime in progress. He wanted to be the hero who would save the day.

It seemed so strange to me. How could we be brothers? I knew intimately that justice didn't work. There were people like me all over the world.

One day, Kostas told me about a twenty-seven-year-old criminal. When this guy was fifteen, he ran away with a teenage girl, leading him to a reformatory for six months. There, he made connections with the underworld.

I knew all too well about going down that road. It's super hard to come back from. Later, this guy was accused of attempted murder, homicide, and several robberies, but he escaped custody shortly before the trial.

He was arrested again and led to the Corfu prison. The following year, he escaped the prison hospital and was arrested again. A few days later, he was taken to Larissa Prison and escaped once more.

The authorities coincidentally found him in a blockade and took him to a psychiatric hospital. Then they tried to transfer him to St. Stephen's Prison, and the bastard escaped again.

Kostas had watched all this from afar and knew the story quite well.

Eventually, the authorities got a lead on where the guy was staying. Kostas learned when the raid would occur and joined his fellow officers at the site. I heard what happened from the news and from the few details Kostas offered upon his return.

Kostas stood at the entrance of the building so as not to draw any unwanted attention. A woman holding more shopping bags than she could manage was about to open the main door. Kostas tried to stop her, but she got scared and screamed.

There was a loud bang, and the whole dilapidated building shook. A man rushed down the stairs with a weapon in hand, along with several grenades. When the man saw Kostas, he grabbed the woman by the hair, yanked her head back, and pulled her close to him.

"Move aside, or the woman's dead."

"Let her go," Kostas told him in a steady voice.

The woman moaned and screamed in hysterics under the man's grip. He hit her in the head, then dragged her toward the door.

"I said, let her go," Kostas ordered.

"What are you? A cop?"

"Look, you don't want to do that." Kostas approached the man as they neared a car parked in the rear of the building. This surprised the guy, so he fired one wild shot and then placed the weapon at the woman's head.

"You need her," Kostas said. "Don't do anything stupid. She's your ticket to freedom." Kostas moved another step closer. "But, she's too loud. Take me instead."

The woman had lost consciousness. The guy released her and turned his weapon on Kostas.

"You got handcuffs?"

Kostas nodded.

"Put them on, hands at the front."

Kostas did as he was told.

"Now get in and drive."

Kostas dropped into the driver's seat, fired up the car, and drove where the guy told him to go.

The officers showing up to raid the place were left without a criminal in the building to apprehend.

Eventually, the authorities put it together and followed the guy's car while Kostas drove. So, the guy took one of the grenades and put it between Kostas's legs.

"If they stop us, you won't live to talk about it," the guy said.

"The sooner you stop and surrender, the easier it'll go for you."

"Cut the bullshit. Shut the fuck up and drive. You'll be the first to die if we don't lose them."

"You understand that this road doesn't lead anywhere but a prison, right?"

"You cops are all the same. If you guys were smart, I wouldn't have escaped so often."

Kostas continued to drive while trying to formulate an escape plan.

"I can't be imprisoned. Do you fucking understand I will always win and escape? I don't give a shit about you or your fucking system. Incompetent cops. Drive faster before I get bored and just fucking kill you for fun. I'm already accused of murder; might as well add to it."

Kostas didn't pay attention to the guy's rant. He remained focused on the road. If he wanted to live, this was his only way out.

In the meantime, I turned on the TV and watched what was happening live. If the asshole hurt my brother, I would make him pay. I remained glued to the TV screen as it all played out.

Kostas drove according to Adrian's instructions. After passing through several neighborhoods and losing most of their tail, they arrived at an old, abandoned train station. They broke into the depot before anyone saw them.

Kostas wondered if this was the end for him. He stopped the car.

The guy in the back seat leaned forward, placing the gun near Kostas's neck.

"I may have done many shitty things, but I have no beef with you. Don't follow me, and you're free to go."

"I can't do that."

The gun pressed into his flesh. "You're such a dickhead."

Something smacked the back of Kostas's head so hard that he lost consciousness. When he opened his eyes, I was with him in the hospital. Kostas had a concussion, but that was it.

"Are you fucking serious?" I asked. "You live your life to the toss of a coin? Why? To catch a bad guy?" I was so upset; my palms were sweaty, and my heart raced.

"Shhh, slow down. My head's going to break."

"If it doesn't break on its own, I can help you out. How could you be such an idiot?" I didn't want him to know I was lost without him. Without him, sooner or later, I'd end up in jail. He was the reason I tried to be clean. He was my good side. If my good side died, then what would be left of me?

The days went by, and Kostas saw it as a personal failure to have let the guy escape. He watched every new development, pissed that the guy was out there somewhere, having escaped again.

"Don't bother with him," I kept telling him, but he didn't seem to give a fuck. He just kept listening to the police radio, searching for anything new.

A few days later, he heard that the guy had been found in the center of Athens. Kostas spoke to several colleagues, and he learned that Adrian —the guy's name—was in an apartment with three hostages.

Within a few hours, Kostas was back on the job. I sat left alone to wait impatiently. I didn't know what to do, so I listened to the police radio as well. From there, I learned that Adrian was live on TV. I turned it on, and then I heard his voice. He said he wanted money, freedom, and drugs.

I knew what building he was in.

I saw where he was.

I got dressed as fast as I could and grabbed a taxi to the area. A large crowd had gathered outside the apartment building. Journalists and passersby stood outside, waiting for new developments. We watched a hostage situation in progress live from the road that was filled with police cruisers.

When I saw my brother, I waved at him. He saw me and smiled. The authorities were trying to make a plan of attack. They had no idea what the guy was capable of or how far he would go to survive. I felt sorry for them. Some people believe in the power of their uniform, but to me, the uniform holds no value. Suppose you can wear the uniform with honor, good for you. If you wear it to be a bully, you're an asshole. In the end, it's not the uniform that makes a cop. It's the man.

Eventually, special forces went upstairs with ropes. They were ready to invade with tear gas. The plan had been decided. But as it turned out, they had no idea what they were doing, and it almost cost my brother's life.

Adrian had placed a grenade in a hostage's pants. When it blew, everyone on the ground covered their heads. Pandemonium ensued as cops ran everywhere. They entered the building with paramedics to check on the injured. I was trying like crazy to get close enough to check on my stupid brother because I knew he would've been right up front.

Since people didn't move out of my way, I pushed and shoved them until I reached the police line. Ambulance sirens wailed all around us. The media assholes had blocked the roads so several ambulances couldn't get closer. When I returned to the closest ambulance, I told them I was a doctor and needed a white coat. Amid the panic, they didn't even think about it—they just handed one over.

I ran for the building, shouting that I was a doctor. That one word was magical. Everyone moved aside for me to pass. At the police line, they let me pass immediately, and I climbed to the second floor of the building.

As I entered the room, I saw a disgusting sight. Blood and human flesh were scattered everywhere. The smell was unbearable. Through the thick smoke, I looked for Kostas. Those who could walk on their own had already come out.

Some people looked like living corpses. I saw a girl with her legs cut off, and another person had lost only one leg. The man missing one leg had a piercing scream.

But where was Kostas?

Then I found him. A kitchen table was on top of him. I removed the table, placed a hand on his neck to check his pulse, and found that my brother was alive.

I shouted his name, but he didn't respond. I knew I shouldn't move him, that I could worsen his injuries, but he had blood on the back of his head, which wasn't good. I couldn't do anything for him. He had to go to the hospital.

What was certain was that the bastard who did this wouldn't escape because he couldn't get rid of me. I wanted to find him and kill him as soon as possible.

I went down to the main floor of the apartment building to avoid the risk of rescue personnel confusing me with Kostas. My hair was a different length, and the only way you could separate us was the earring in my ear.

The police were helping the paramedics with the injured. Ambulances were still blocked farther up the road.

I watched them put my brother in an ambulance with a police officer, then sped away. I remained behind, still in my doctor's coat, hoping to glimpse Adrian. His life had to end at my hands. He'd hurt my brother. He'd made it my business now.

I found the ambulance that contained Adrian. He had been hurt badly by the arresting officers. I jumped up and glared down at the beast of a man. How I could be so lucky to get a private audience with Adrian was fate. I stood in the open doorway of the ambulance and told the cop standing nearby that I needed to examine him in private, and then I closed the door.

After locating a powerful sedative, I injected Adrian. The man nearly passed out on me. Before he was completely out, I took a jar with some unidentifiable liquid and forced the entire thing down the guy's throat. He had trouble swallowing, but the sedative made him an easy victim.

It wasn't long before he was choking to death. The truth is, I didn't like seeing him like this, but didn't he do the same to Kostas? I looked away from my handiwork after the asshole stopped breathing, grabbed some gauze to appear professional, then exited the ambulance keeping my head down.

I closed the door behind me. The cop asked how the fucker was doing.

"I injected him with a sedative for the pain. He'll be quiet for a while. I'm going to check on the others." Then I stepped away.

I removed my robe when I got out of sight of the ambulances, then ran to my brother's superior officer.

"Mr. Eleftheriou."

"Kostas?" He stared at me as if he saw a ghost.

I shook my head. "I'm his brother."

"He has a brother? He never told me."

"Where is he?"

"They're taking him to the General Hospital—"

I didn't hear any more as I was already running.

It took me ages to get through traffic to the main road and then to the hospital. The gathered crowds made the situation worse. When I got inside, I was directed to the doctor who was treating my brother.

Kostas was already in surgery. The doctor informed me that his condition was serious. The blow to the head caused extensive damage. The operation would be crucial to his life.

I couldn't wait. I felt helpless. It was the first time that killing or hitting someone couldn't get me what I wanted.

From the news, I learned that the suspect died in the back of the ambulance. They didn't say anything about a new suspect dressed as a doctor. Maybe it was convenient for them not to have a new scandal. If the media learned that the suspect was murdered with all those officers standing around, the police would lose any respect they still clung to.

After the operation, Kostas was in a coma. I stayed with him day and night. I couldn't stand being at home alone. The hospital had once again become my home. Only now, we weren't young children playing hide and seek in the corridors.

I thought of Katerina and how good it would be to find her.

Thoughts of how my life had turned out saddened me. Losing contact with Katerina, my brother in a coma, and Kiki being used and abused.

The familiar smell of the hospital had awakened my childhood memories. Buried feelings rose to the surface—abandonment, contempt, and negligence.

Why was life such a fucked up ride?

Chapter 13

Kostas recovered and came back home. Although he wasn't the same man. His failure to apprehend the suspect and his close call to death had cost him a lot emotionally. He was on sick leave, but he didn't want to go back to the special forces, and he didn't want to get a new job. He sat at home all day looking at the wall or the television. Only when I fought with him would he decide to go for a walk with his cop friends. He didn't talk to me either. I had to force him to speak to me.

I decided to get a job since he was on sick leave and driving me nuts. They didn't dare fire him. They just had him on leave, like the garbage you don't have the time or the will to throw away or hide under your rug.

I found a job at a company that made raw materials for bakeries. I had shaved and removed my earrings in an attempt to act like a gentleman. The mask of kindness and goodness was a great success. I wasn't too familiar with office work, so they hired me to be their debt collector—people late on making payments. They gave me a seminar on how to behave with these customers so as not to offend them but to be persuasive and polite simultaneously.

My boss, Mr. Kalimeris, was a kind gentleman. He seemed helpful to everyone who worked for him. He often put his hand in his pocket and was often generous. As soon as he hired me, he gave me an advance of fifteen days' salary. It seemed so unreal for my life so far. Fortunately, I was doing well. I had never done this job before but I learned quickly and did what they asked me to do. If anyone was talking to me a little strange, I tried to suck it up. I had to do this for Kostas. Otherwise, we'd be thrown into the streets.

I was late getting back one day. Everyone else had left, and I had to hand over money to the boss. I entered the well-kept reception area, passed the warehouse where everything was permanently covered with flour and sugar, and went up on the loft. Kalimeris's office was there. All the lights were turned off, and I could barely see where I was going. I knocked on the door. No one answered. I took the liberty to open it and stepped inside.

"Mr. Kalimeris?" I whispered.

Next to the office, he had a door that was always closed. Today, it was open. A faint light shone from behind the door. Curiosity made one foot move in front of the other as I needed to see what was hidden behind that door. I eased out the knife I always had in my pocket and clutched it tightly. I came as close as I could without stepping into the small amount of light washing the floor yellow.

A female voice pleaded something I couldn't make out. A masculine whisper responded.

I eased closer.

"Please give us some time. I know I should have already paid you, I know. Keep these earrings. They're gold, I swear to you. My husband gave them to me."

"I've already given you more time than I usually allow," Mr. Kalimeris said harshly.

"The bakery doesn't do so well," the woman said, her tone dejected.

"We recently renovated to allow for my niece, and I didn't calculate the costs properly. But I give you my word, and when Cleo gives her word, she means it. By the end of the month, you will be paid." Cleo's voice trembled at the last word.

Could it be the Mrs. Cleo I knew? For real?

A chair scraped the floor. They were getting to their feet and would leave through the door I stood at.

I slipped away and hid behind the sacks of flour.

I watched Mrs. Cleo descend the stairs.

Seeing her for the first time after so many years of hatred, I didn't feel like I expected. On the contrary, it seemed she was no longer as arrogant as she used to be. She didn't have that stupid pride that got on my nerves. She left terrified, with her head down, so no one would see her.

I remained hidden for a while. Then, I slipped out of the side exit without making a noise.

I urgently wanted to speak to Kostas. Only he would understand me.

"I'm telling you the truth," I pleaded.

"And what was she doing there?"

"Hey, man, I recognized her. The only difference was she had gotten older."

"Will you help her?"

"Help her?" I gasped for breaths, swallowed, then asked, "Are you fucking kidding me? I was thinking of hurting her somehow, not helping her." I clenched my fists. "That filthy bitch. Because of her, I went to the reformatory. I could be dead now."

"That was a long time ago. You've changed. You became a better person. She may have changed, too. Doesn't she deserve a second chance?"

Kostas was so naïve. He always believed people had a good side, whereas I saw the opposite. People have a dark side that reveals itself effortlessly. Doing something terrible without thinking about the consequences is easier than doing the right thing or the hard thing.

I couldn't give her a second chance. I'd waited years for revenge, and my time had finally come. Why would I let it go? Why squander this chance?

When I went to work the next day, I went straight to Mr. Kalimeris's office to deliver the cash from the previous day.

"Good morning."

"Good morning. Why didn't you come yesterday?"

"I came, but because you had someone in your office, I remained discreet, staying back to offer you privacy."

"People in my office?"

"Yes, a lady."

He eyed me momentarily, then lit his cigarette and propped his feet on his desk.

"Do you want to make extra money?" He studied my face. "You aren't like the others. You're more like me. I can see it in your look, the way you act. I've seen you watching over your shoulder as if someone's following you." He puffed on his cigarette, then blew out the smoke. "Do you have trouble with the law?" He asked this question as if it were something casual.

I had recently felt that Fats was watching me, but I didn't expect it to be so obvious.

"No, sir, I have no issues with the law." I met his gaze without wavering. I currently had no trouble with law enforcement, so I was speaking the truth.

He watched my every move. I didn't know if that was the right answer, but it was the only one he was getting.

After a long, uncomfortable pause, I asked, "Can I do something for you to make this extra money you spoke of?" I wanted this to end, as I already felt pretty stupid standing there as if I were passing an exam.

"I think you can, but I'll need this to remain confidential." His eyes were unwavering.

"You can tell me," I told him without wanting to listen. "Think of me as a secret keeper."

"That old bitch who was here yesterday has borrowed money from me. And now she mocks me, making fun of me while promising to give it back."

"She borrowed from you?"

"My boy, if I waited for money from the trade, I would have closed my business years ago. I didn't hire you by accident. I know some of your story, and I'm sorry. I feel most sorry for your brother. But because you have guts, I want you to go one step further. I want you to intimidate her. If you manage to get me my money, you'll get a hefty share of it yourself." He spoke in a clear, low voice. "I know you want revenge. I can smell it. One carnivore understands the anger of the other. But in this jungle, the law is the strongest. If someone had the misfortune to be born on the wrong side, then the beasts eat him. Cleo is an old witch, and every orphan who passes through her hands has been made a slave. She once gave me a girl as a form of payment as she didn't have the money, so the girl paid her bill by working it off."

"What has she done with all the money she's borrowed?"

"She's a gambler. She plays cards. Gambling devours your soul until it has nothing left to eat, and then it goes after the people close to you."

The more he told me, the more I felt an internal rage. I didn't want to intimidate her, to get her to pay what she owed. I wanted to kill her, to see her beg for mercy. But what was better? The death of her body or the slow death of her soul? Maybe I should plan it differently and make her suffer more.

"I will get your money back. I'll need time." I smiled. "I have something in mind."

He smiled back at me, then puffed on his cigarette again as I exited his office.

How could he know so much about me? Where did he learn about my brother?

For a start, I decided to go to her bakery. My little visit would surely surprise her. It didn't take long to get there. I stepped inside the bakery and saw Helen behind the counter. As I approached and she recognized me, I detected fear in her eyes—she was afraid of me.

"What would you like?" she asked, a slight tremble in her voice.

I couldn't keep my eyes off her. She had transformed into a stunning woman. Who would've imagined that?

"Are you afraid of me?" I asked her in a calm voice.

"Excuse me?"

"Did I change that much?"

"Nikos? With short hair and clothes like that, you are unrecognizable. What are you doing in our neighborhood?"

"I wanted to see you," I told her, staring into her eyes. Surprised, she played with an errant strand of curly hair while leaning on the bench.

"I was wondering what happened to you," she whispered, as if afraid someone would hear us.

"Where is she?"

"Who, my aunt? She'll be late, don't worry."

Helen stared at me, her eyes roving over my chest, my flat stomach. I recalled she was something of a slut at a young age, but this wasn't the right time.

"I'm so happy to see you," I whispered back. "I'll come again soon. Don't tell her anything about me."

"Are you crazy? I would never mention your name." She winked at me as I was leaving.

Perhaps I misread her. Maybe it wasn't fear I'd detected when we first saw each other. Maybe it was a surprise.

I knew it was only a matter of time before things would work out how I wanted.

I went back to work after that. I couldn't go home right away as Kostas would suspect something was up, and I couldn't hide from him.

When I returned home that afternoon, he was there waiting for me, glaring from the moment I stepped inside.

"I did nothing wrong," I shouted, storming into the kitchen. "Stop looking at me like that."

He stayed in the living room, which was his tactic. He didn't have to say anything to break me. He just looked at me with that critical, inquisitive look—a particular stern look that irritated me so much.

"What the fuck do you want?" I yelled at him as I moved through the living room toward my bedroom. But he kept staring at me, still dressed in yesterday's clothes.

"I know you're planning something," he shouted at me from the living room. "I feel it."

I didn't say anything. I didn't want to speak. I didn't want him to know. It wasn't his business.

The next day, I passed by the bakery after ensuring that Mrs. Cleo wasn't there.

Helen was working as usual. When she saw me, she started as I moved close to her.

"What do you think?" I asked. "Will you be able to leave tonight?" I squeezed her into a corner. I felt her heart beating through her ribcage. I stroked her cheek and then left her abruptly. "I'll be here at eleven," I said as I stepped outside.

I was never emotionally interested in women. I saw them as human beings who will use you, and then when they don't need you, they leave you. I had them in my life only to satisfy my needs, whether it was sex, money, help, or anything I could get from them. For me, they were a means to fulfill a purpose.

So, Helen would help me with my revenge.

From the moment I first met her, I could tell she was into me. She would come to the bakery to see me, making excuses to do so. She would just look at me—not my brother, me—but I didn't want to take advantage of her. In fact, if they caught us, they would kick us out of the house. The whole neighborhood knew of her accomplishments.

Helen, the daughter of a woman who had an affair, was left to the care of her aunt, Mrs. Cleo, when Helen's parents divorced, and neither could care for her. The more Mrs. Cleo tried to control her, the more Helen found a way to do as she pleased. Helen wasn't just an innocent little girl, no matter what her aunt thought of her.

For me, I was only interested in Katerina, my floating piece of wood in the ocean of abandonment. She never betrayed me, and they took her away from me. When Kostas was looking for our parents, he was also looking for her, but she was nowhere to be found. It was as if the earth had opened up and swallowed her whole. At some point, however, our paths would meet again, I was sure of it—if I didn't die in the meantime.

When I got home, Kostas was waiting for me.

"Will you go out at all?" I asked him. "Will you have a life beyond sitting at home, or will you sit here for decades more, rotting?"

"I'm in no mood."

"I can't see you here like this all the time. Go out, have fun, find a woman."

"Leave me alone, and just tell me how your day went."

"Don't change the subject. Get off the fucking sofa and take a bath."

He didn't answer.

I worried about him. A darkness had begun to surround him. It felt like he had taken a piece of me and made it a part of him. This wasn't good.

I left him in the living room and went into the kitchen to get him something to eat. He had stopped eating, too, the dishes stacked untouched in our cupboards. If he didn't fix this shit soon, I would have to take him to a doctor. I could never imagine I would end up being his dad.

I cleaned the house and did all the chores while Kostas slept on the couch, the TV blaring.

Quietly, once the place was relatively clean, I left. An hour later, I parked at the front of the bakery. I hid behind a car and waited to see Helen. When she stepped outside looking for me, I pushed off the wall I leaned against and signaled her.

She got on my bike, and we left as fast as we could. I took her to the marina, where we sat on a bench.

"You're so beautiful tonight," I told her as if I meant it.

"Thank you," she replied, smiling sweetly. I noticed a weird look on her face, and she stared into my eyes. "Why did you come back to the bakery?" After a moment, she glanced down at her hands as she fidgeted with her fingers nervously.

"You didn't want me to?"

"I didn't ask you that."

"I never forgot about you," I told her and held her hand.

"I'm sure I was the only one who could tell the difference between you and your brother."

"How?"

"It's just that when I saw you, my heart danced. There's something dark about you." She smiled.

I took advantage of the moment and hugged her. She smelled so nice, but her weakness didn't fit my plan.

"Will you stay?" she asked with disarming simplicity.

"Why not?" I replied, tightening my hug. We spent a lot of time in silence. Then she stroked my hair.

"When you were away, my aunt became suspicious of your brother and was chasing him nonstop. He was patient as he had no choice. He wasn't the guy who could make it on the streets. One night, thieves broke into the bakery and stole the cash register. She was sure Kostas had something to do with it. They disgraced him, threw his clothes out, and our uncle beat him. Kostas defended himself as much as he could but didn't know how to protect himself from a man at such a young age. They locked him out of the house, beaten, broken, and crying."

Rage morphed to fury as I listened to Helen speak. The raw anger grew inside me like cancer. I thought I couldn't hate that woman more, but I was wrong.

Helen took a cigarette out of her pocket and lit it.

"You're smoking?"

"I'm not innocent." She gave me a look.

"I just didn't expect it from you."

She inhaled, exhaled, and then continued. "That night, I went out secretly as I had done countless times. I found Kostas crying in an alleyway. I dragged him to a safe place, where he passed out, then I ran to my best friend for help. But my friend was drunk as fuck and wouldn't give me his car keys unless I returned the favor. I took his car and took Kostas to the hospital. I left him there with some of his details on a piece of paper. I had to come back before they discovered me missing. Kostas didn't rat me out, nor them, and they accepted him back, but he was not himself." She puffed on her cigarette again, then looked away from me. "The first night he came back, I slipped into his room and made love to him, but in my mind, I was making love to you. We never talked about it." She fell silent.

"Why are you telling me this?"

She snapped her head to glare at me. "You don't understand? I made love to you." She flicked the cigarette away, climbed on top of me, and kissed me hard like I was the last man on earth. Piece by piece, she took off my clothes. I didn't resist. I gave myself up to her until it was time to take her home. I had her smell all over me. It was one of the most honest nights I've ever had. I was Nikos for a while, and it felt good.

Kostas was asleep on the couch when I got home. The sofa had become his second skin. I was happy he was sleeping as I didn't want to talk to him about Helen.

I couldn't get up in the morning. The previous night was wonderful—the first time I felt happiness in a long time—if ever. However, there was a shadow of sadness. Something about it made me feel like I had disappointed Katerina. She was somewhere in the world waiting for me. I should not deviate from my purpose. I had to stay focused on revenge and my need for Katerina. These two things kept me alive. If I left Katerina and vengeance behind, there would be no return. The darkness would sweep away my soul.

Sometimes, the image of my dead mother came to my mind. She haunted me no matter how much I wanted to remove her from my thoughts. When I was drunk, she spoke to me. She never told me anything good. Only insults, repeating over and over that I wasn't capable of anything. I was born evil, even though I killed Takis for her sake. But it didn't matter how she felt about me. I enjoyed burning that son of a bitch. He deserved it.

Another day had passed, and I was set to meet Helen again. Mrs. Cleo was napping, so our timing was perfect. We met a little farther down the street from the bakery, and I couldn't keep my hands off her. It was like Helen's entire body invited me to touch, kiss, and taste it. I had lost my mind with lust.

Because Mrs. Cleo was napping, we returned to the bakery. We had half an hour at least. I kissed her and undressed her while knocking everything off the counter. As flour floated in the air around us, we made love again. It was like a dream I didn't want to wake from. Even her breath made my body shiver. She whispered in my ear that she would be mine forever, only mine, and it was the first time I believed something someone had told me.

Then we heard Mrs. Cleo.

"Helen, is that you?"

"I have to go," I whispered.

"I don't want you to leave. I want to stay with you."

"We'll meet in the evening," I told her and left like someone was chasing me. I had to be more focused on my goal. In the evening, I would implement my plan.

Unfortunately, Kostas was waiting for me upon my return.

"What are you up to?" he asked.

"Wow, he talks." I acted stunned.

"Say it."

"Say what?" I stopped by my bedroom door, glaring at him.

"I know you too well. I know when you're up to something. I can smell it."

"Do yourself a favor and stop harassing me," I said, then entered my room. Being in my room was the safest option. When I was involved with Fats, Kostas knew something was wrong before anyone else. He observed me and could tell from my expressions and how I behaved that something was going on. Unbeknownst to me, I changed somehow. I just couldn't understand how. Now, when I think about it, maybe guilt changed me because I didn't want to hurt Helen during my revenge on Mrs. Cleo. Destiny seemed to haunt me. Maybe I didn't deserve to be happy.

That night, when I met her, I told her I would come into some serious money or have to leave the area. I had old debts with some punks from the reformatory that needed to be paid. When Helen heard this, she cried. She told me she would do anything to have me in her life.

A week later, after meeting every night, Helen brought me

money. She looked me in the eyes and said, "Honey, I did it. I've been trying to see her put the money in the safe for days, and she finally did. Cleo opened it and murmured the numbers. As soon as she left, I opened and removed this." She held a pack of cash so I could see it. "Take it. Please tell me it's enough for you to stay."

She opened the pack. Inside, several thousand were tied together with a rubber band.

"I didn't have time to count it," she said with a smile as she placed the whole pack in the palm of my hand.

Pity was a new emotion for me. At that moment, it was all I felt. I felt sorry for her, too, because she wouldn't be able to change my plan. I took the money with a smile, counted it, and put it in my pockets. I hugged her, kissed her hard, and caressed her silky hair, which smelled of orange blossoms. With my tongue, I licked her earlobe and felt her shudder with lust.

Then I whispered in her ear. "Thank you. Your selfless act shows how much you care for me. No one would ever do that for me, but you did. I'm closer to paying off my debts now, but this isn't enough." I touched her arms softly.

"I want whatever you want," she whispered back. "You drive me crazy, and I can't resist you."

She removed her clothes right there, looking like an angel in the sea of darkness. The two of us made love beneath the stars. Her body was mine, and I had started to take her soul, too.

The next morning, I took the money to my boss.

"You're late," he said, dropping into the large chair behind his desk.

"It takes time to get this cash without leaving a trace or resorting to violence."

"How much you got there?"

"Several thousand."

"Time is running out."

"How is time running out?"

"I'm just tired of that bitch and her lies, her games."

"Give me fifteen days, I'll get the rest. I'll take everything from her."

"You have seven days."

I stared at him a moment. "I need a minimum of ten."

"If you don't get results, I'll burn her business to the ground. I'll burn all of them."

"No, if I don't get the rest for you, I'll burn her myself."

He frowned at me. "You got the guts for that kind of shit?"

"You have no idea. Things aren't always how they seem." I bowed respectfully and left. I worked menial tasks throughout the rest of the day, then went home.

I had a problem, and I knew it. I didn't know how to get more money out of Mrs. Cleo's place of business. Helen was a great resource, but she was sitting in the room with the safe all day. Cleo probably figured out she was short of money and didn't know what had happened yet. I met Helen every night with empty hands and was short of time.

On the morning of the seventh day, my boss called me. I entered his office with my head down, not knowing what to expect from him.

"Your time's up," he told me. He paced behind his desk, smoking his cigarette with trembling hands.

Why was he nervous?

"Please," I begged. "I need more time."

"Leave," he said in a firm tone.

I couldn't understand what had happened. He had changed so much from our previous meeting. Going down the stairs, I saw two tough-looking guys asking for him.

His deadline was due.

I left the building, running to meet Helen. Things had become too dangerous, and I had put Helen in the middle of the situation—my innocent Helen. I walked around the exterior of the bakery until she saw me and came out. I signaled her and hid behind a tree, where I waited.

"This may be the last time I see you. I'll be dead if I stay any longer. I need the money right away, or I have to disappear."

The look of shock on her face told me how she felt.

Her voice came out with difficulty. "Today?"

"Yes, today," I replied as I wiped away the tears that had started to flow from her sweet eyes. It was the first time someone was crying for me. The first time someone cared about me was if I lived or died, if I stayed or left.

"Don't cry, please," I told her, kissing her salty tears. Her skin smelled so lovely.

"I know we haven't been together long, but I love you. I genuinely love you. I love your smile, how you treat me, how you look at me, and how you stroke my hair. You are the only one who feels me, who understands me. I will love you until the end of time, and if you leave, my soul will die." Her kiss was strong and full of passion.

I didn't expect those words and didn't know how to respond, so I put on my dark mask again.

"I love you, too. I can't stand living without you." Wait, were these words coming from me or the mask? Was I actually able to feel love?

She clung to me like I was a life raft. "I'm afraid," she whispered. "I can't stand the thought of you getting hurt. I will take all of her money and give it to you. She doesn't need it the way you do. I will help you, and everything will be fine."

"Should I return tonight when she's asleep?" I asked.

She nodded, eased out of my arms, wiped her eyes, and trudged away. I stayed to watch her cross the street. Was it truly possible for someone to love me? She didn't know me. She had no idea what kind of person I was. My mother hadn't loved me. Kiki had said that I didn't deserve love. Perhaps she was right. How does someone love a man who feels nothing other than hatred? There was definitely something there for Katerina, but I could not define or categorize it. And, of course, what I felt was, for little Katerina, the memory of her. What if I saw her older, damaged from life?

I didn't want to go home. The last thing I needed was to be around Kostas while he asked me many stupid questions.

I don't remember how many hours passed before it was night. Had I fallen asleep? Someone asked me if I needed anything, but I brushed him off. He threw me a coin and walked away, mumbling something under his breath. I fell asleep and had a strange dream.

Something about a black dove and snapping its neck. As I killed it, the bird squirmed in my hands, and I laughed. I remember opening my eyes, knocked out of the dream by the bird's squeal.

I told myself everything would go well. My plan would work. I would give the money to my boss, and Mrs. Cleo would be broke. Then I could be with Helen. Cleo would end up having an accident, and then I'd live with Helen and my brother, and we'd work in the bakery together, happily ever after. It was the first reasonable life plan I'd ever had. Maybe I was feeling something akin to love.

The time had finally come. Helen found me where she had left me. I smoked as I walked in nervous circles around her. I lit one cigarette after another as I had a bad feeling that I was trying to get rid of. Helen hugged me and held me close.

"I want the time to freeze and not to pass a single minute." She nestled her head into my neck. "If I can't get the money, take me with you. We'll leave together."

Life and death were like a chain to me; I was just a small black ring. Each time I was in danger, I moved toward death. When the danger was gone, I moved toward life. Although, my black ring was invariably always listed on the side of death. I had nothing to lose, nothing to gain.

"Everything will be fine. You go in first, and I'll come in behind you."

I gently pulled away from her. She stared into my eyes and nodded. Her white dress fluttered like an angel when she ran back toward the bakery.

I waited for her to get behind the counter to resume work, and then I'd go in.

Ten minutes later, when I entered the bakery, Helen wasn't behind the counter.

Where did she go?

Voices were coming from upstairs. Mrs. Cleo was awake. I had to get upstairs before the neighborhood woke up. I climbed the stairs and strode silently to the apartment door, trying to listen to who was with Mrs. Cleo.

"Little whore," Mrs. Cleo shouted. "Tell me what you want the money for. Say it. Who knew all this time that I was raising a snake."

Mrs. Cleo's shouting unnerved me and made me clench my fists

Furniture moved, scraping the floor. Helen's crying was loud enough to be heard in the hallway.

I couldn't stand it anymore. Helen was no longer Cleo's niece. She was mine.

"Tell me," Mrs. Cleo shouted. "How much have you stolen over the years?" Mrs. Cleo did something that sounded like she spit. "You ungrateful whore. I fed you, and this is the thanks I get?"

I heard the distinctive sound of someone slapping flesh.

"Let me go, you stupid bitch," Helen screamed. "You only ever use people. You're a gambler and an alcoholic. I've endured your shit for too many years, but I can't stand it anymore. Let me go."

I wasn't going to let her hit her again—ever. I reared back and kicked the door, smashing it inward.

Mrs. Cleo was holding Helen by her hair, pulling her head back.

"Let her go, bitch!" I shouted.

Mrs. Cleo jerked her head in my direction. "You?" She seemed to breathe that one word out. "What are you doing here, scumbag? Didn't jail clear your head? They should have kept you inside where you could die like a dog." Mrs. Cleo glanced at Helen, then back at me, realization dawning on her features. "You made her do it, didn't you? She wouldn't have done this on her own. She only knows how to fuck anything with a cock." Then Mrs. Cleo slapped Helen's face so hard that her neck snapped backward.

"I will kill you if you slap her again."

I lunged forward and grabbed at her. The hatred in her eyes couldn't compare to the hatred I had in me, the hatred that consumed me.

Mrs. Cleo was able to avoid my grasp by releasing Helen.

"You want the money?" she asked. "Is that it? Is that what this is about? You're here to rob Mrs. Cleo." She moved to the wall and dropped in front of the safe. "Take it all," she said as she opened the safe. She only had a few thousand.

I grabbed her neck when she reached out to hand it to me.

"Where are you hiding the rest? Speak. I know you have more. Where is it all?" I squeezed her neck hard, her eyes opening wide. She batted at me, fighting for a breath.

Helen came up behind me.

"Leave her alone, please. You're scaring me." She genuinely sounded frightened.

That calmed me down. Slowly, I released my grip. Mrs. Cleo dropped to her knees, a hand on her throat as she gasped for air.

I had wanted so badly to watch the life ebb out of Mrs. Cleo while staring into her eyes. But if I killed her, I would have failed. I wouldn't know where the rest of the money was, and Helen would be a witness to a murder.

To survive this, I had to control my anger.

"Bring us the rest of the money," I shouted at Cleo.

She nodded from the floor, coughed, and scrambled to move into the next room.

I made the mistake of waiting. I wanted to soothe Helen and calm her after she saw a snippet of my dark side. At some point, she'd see more of it because how much can someone hide their true self? How long could I pretend? Eventually, the mask cracks.

Mrs. Cleo came back into the room, a grin on her face.

"I have it here, in my pocket." She patted it. She slipped her hand inside and withdrew a gun.

By the way, she held that weapon, it seemed like it was her first time.

"Get the hell out of here. Get away from me, and stay away from her. You only bring disaster and misery. This time, stay the fuck away."

"Auntie, please drop the gun."

"You don't even know how a gun works. Just give me the money, and I'll leave. I'll disappear. You'll never see me again."

"You're never getting a cent from me," she shouted.

I took a step toward her. "Lower that thing before someone gets hurt." I took another step.

"Nikos," Helen pleaded from behind me. "We'd better leave." She tugged on my arm.

"Don't come any closer," Mrs. Cleo said, her voice trembling, matching the shaking gun in her hands. "I'll fucking shoot you."

"Do you think I care? Do you think it matters to me? Do it then, kill me and set me free." I raised my hands, spreading my arms wide. "Come on, don't hesitate, get me out of this miserable life. But then you'll be like me, a murderer. Your hands will be stained with blood."

"Shut up," she screamed.

"You're worse than a murderer because you murder them while they're still alive. You exploit children. You steal their souls. You rape them of their dreams of ever possibly having a real family. Shame on you, you disgusting piece of shit, woman. I should just bash in your face, and then—"

The gun fired.

Time stopped.

I'd been ready to welcome the redemption of the bullet, but I flinched and recoiled when the weapon fired so close to me.

There was a ringing in my ears, but I could still hear someone shouting *No* repeatedly.

Mrs. Cleo had thrown the gun to the floor, her hands covering her mouth while she stared behind me.

I turned around to see Helen. The bullet had missed me but hit her.

Mrs. Cleo had shot Helen.

I ran to Helen and took her in my arms as blood spurted from her mouth, and her body went into spasms.

"You'll be fine," I whispered and held her tight.

"My love," she gasped. "Get out of here." Helen coughed. "Get the money, save your life. I love you to death, Nikos." She struggled for another breath, then gasped her last one onto my cheek.

I closed her dead eyes, then mine. The darkness welcomed me in my moment of despair.

Mrs. Cleo seemed paralyzed with shock, curled up in a ball on the floor in front of her gun, shaking with tears.

I grabbed the weapon and placed it in Helen's hand. She wiped her eyes with her free hand and stared at me in puzzlement. I raised Helen's gun hand, aimed it at Mrs. Cleo's face, then forced the trigged back.

The bullet hit her between the eyes. She didn't have a second to react to what I was doing before she was dead, too.

With a plastic bag over my hand, I searched the house for money as fast as I could. She had a stash hidden in a Bible. Once I had everything I could find, I left through the back door.

Surely, someone would have called the police after the shooting.

I had to get to work to give my boss the money. At this point, I was acting like a robot, keeping thoughts of Helen from my mind by staying busy and active.

I arrived fifteen minutes later as all roads were favorable, but I arrived too late.

Firefighters had blocked the road.

The company had caught fire. I lumbered home, barely able to walk. Failure covered every centimeter of my body, and I could barely breathe.

Kostas wasn't in the living room, which was good as I didn't want to talk to him.

I had thought that revenge would fill me with joy, but all I felt was a large hole in my heart. I had been dreaming of killing Mrs. Cleo for so many years, and yet, I didn't feel happy now that she was dead.

There was no relief. I wasn't free.

Helen was dead.

Killed because of me, which was something I didn't want to think about.

Helen was dead. She was collateral damage.

I got a bottle of whisky and drank as much as possible to feel nothing. I didn't know what else I could do. Helen was dead.

That night, it played over and over in my head. The unjust death, her sacrifice. For me? Was it worth dying for me? And she loved me that much?

There was no one left.

Nothing else mattered anymore.

She was dead, and I was without her.

Chapter 14

IN THE MORNING, I woke up with an incredible headache. I turned on the TV to see what the news was reporting. The first news was the fire at my company and the great loss of the company's owner. Shortly before the news ended, they spoke of two bodies found in Kaminia. The investigation was ongoing, but the media reported it as a murder or suicide.

I didn't want to admit it then—if ever—but I had feelings for Helen. I missed her.

From that point on, my life was an empty, vicious cycle. I couldn't stay in a job. I blamed everything on everyone else, and I was blamed for everything. Sadness was a permanent roommate of my soul.

Helen's loss haunted me. Emptiness, darkness, sorrow, and often, for the first time in my life, guilt. I missed her so much. The void was unbearable. When it happened, I chose to move on, as I would do, but it remained under my skin, festering. At times, I wanted to die, to not live like a parasite, but I was a coward.

I hung a noose and climbed on a chair but couldn't dare kick it out from under me and end it. Then I just drank until I had illusions that

Helen was alive. I held her in my arms, looked her in the eyes, and made love to her. Then she had that glass look on her face, the stare of death, and I was terrified again. I came violently back to life, to the truth, to reality.

Kostas was better, and he wasn't home all the time. He told me they'd accepted him back into the police force. That was great for him, as I sometimes thought he would leave his skin on the couch.

Maybe the positive change in Kostas's life gave me courage.

Of course, with my brother back working at the police station, I should do my best to avoid trouble.

I changed countless jobs until I ended up as a security officer. It was one of the worst choices I've made in my life. The wolf to guard the sheep. At first, they put me in easy positions, but as soon as they saw that I could almost smell the criminals coming, they quickly gave me a more responsible position. There was no way I could get people to like me. We had a typical smell, a particular nature.

Although, I just didn't want to disappoint Kostas. He was the last person on earth who felt something for me. Whatever it was, he felt, however remote, I didn't want it to be lost because of something I did.

Everything seemed to be going well … until it wasn't.

Now it's time to tell you how I ended up here.

I didn't want to speak of it, but I was trapped here. I know it isn't an excuse, but that's exactly what happened.

After Helen's death and my mental death, I decided to leave all the darkness behind. I was trying to avoid trouble because I never wanted to take Kostas down with me. Kostas, who had finally gotten off the couch and restarted his life. Sure, there was the other side to it. Whenever I was late, drunk, or smoked weed, I had a cop at my house—the brother. It was an endless barrage of control and quarrels as if I was under house arrest—who knows, maybe I was. He loved checking on me and thought of himself as my savior.

Although I kept trying to find Katerina, I had turned a page in my life. I was looking for atonement, but I couldn't find it. All I found was a dead end everywhere. I had also made Kostas look for her, but he found nothing. It was as if she had completely vanished and died in a ditch somewhere, and no one ever found her.

I lived a quiet life with the mask of a law-abiding citizen screwed on tight. Of course, in the depths of my soul, there was still one account open, one unpaid account.

The death of Fats.

I tried to leave him behind, but his image nagged at my consciousness. Revenge hadn't given me the taste of sweet nectar I'd expected, only emptiness. On the other hand, I could make a fresh start if this cycle was closed.

I was like a robot every day. I did precisely the same things with minimal variations. I had friends—no girlfriends—only some deceivers who were even worse than me, while Kostas was my everything.

One day, the administration put me in charge of a small bank's security. The bank wasn't the greatest, and according to several sources, they had money laundering issues, hence the increased security.

Since my life was one monotonous day after another, boring as hell, I preferred to work night shifts—the night always suited me better. One morning, just before dawn, I bumped into a familiar face when my shift was over.

"Nikos?" Peter stepped in front of me, blocking my way. "What the hell happened?" he asked, sizing up my uniform. "How the hell did you get so lost?"

At first, I had a hard time recognizing him.

"Peter?" I said, my voice cracking with disbelief. "My, how you've changed."

The rich boy of the reformatory, always in for illegal bets and races, and the one who supplied me with drugs. Nothing about the man before me reminded me of the unfortunate guy I once knew. He wore a suit, had cleaned up nicely, and was tidy. He seemed to have popped out of GQ Magazine.

"Dude, I never expected to see you as a cop. Look at this uniform."

"Oh, I'm not a cop. I'm a security guard. Although, the higher-ups prefer the term, security officer."

"You? Wow, so what does your job entail?"

"Nothing specifically." I glanced over his shoulder, then watched the street momentarily, hoping he'd change the subject.

"I always wondered how you managed to get out of there. Was it some golden connection, or did you pay someone off?"

I fixed my gaze back on him. "Neither."

"Come on, you're going to shit me after all these years?" He laughed and nudged me like we were still juvenile buddies like yesterday.

"Well, Peter, it's been great. So glad I saw you, and we had a chance to reconnect. I have to go and catch the bus." I slapped his shoulder, friendly-like, then hurried away. I wasn't in the mood to continue the conversation or talk about the past. There was nothing left to say.

He shouted after me. "We should meet up again. For old time's sake."

I answered with a wave over my shoulder, hoping it was the last time I saw him.

This short meeting brought all the darkness back for me. A lot of bad memories awoke in me like a monster that had been sleeping for years and woke hungry. The thing would consume my soul if I didn't feed whatever it was.

As I returned home, pictures ran through my mind, images I couldn't eliminate. An image of me trembling and naked, defenseless on the reformatory floor. Another image of all the deaths of revenge, the fights for no reason in the dining room, the screams of teenagers locked in confinement, the guards playing God as if they were some sort of punisher of justice.

Everything was buried in my subconsciousness, like a poison that enters the body and becomes a part of it. There's no medicine to erase memories, and there's no vaccine.

With my demons encircling me, I felt the need for revenge again. Someone had to be punished for my condition. But apart from Fats, no one was left.

Maybe I was the problem.

I wondered what happened to all of my roommates. I hoped they were living just as miserably as I was. From the time we were born, we didn't deserve redemption. They had gone to the outside world, or did they continue their careers in prison?

The bus arrived, and I got on. We were a mass of people crammed next to each other like cattle headed to the slaughter. We exchanged strange looks, accidental touches, odors, germs, and diseases. Sweaty human skin made me nauseous, especially in the summer. Of course, I could take a taxi, but I had to pay attention to my money and only spend the cash I made from my job. Mrs. Cleo's money was well hidden in a safe place.

Sometimes, I felt the eyes of others on me. I was sure people were talking about me, but I didn't care. The more I avoided looking and acting uninterested, the more people pointed at me and commented.

After getting off the bus, I went home and had a shower. I let the water run for a long time as if it would clean the stench of my soul.

Every night at ten, I was at my job. Throughout my shifts, I often saw drug addicts, dealers, whores, and their pimps. Police officers did patrols, taking bribes to look the other way. There were lookouts, thieves, alcoholics vomiting, people arguing, and all the things that the darkness of the night tried to hide. There were sideways glances at my back, whispers, gestures—they saw me as an opponent.

What they didn't know was that I was a wolf in sheep's clothing.

The lowlifes of the night didn't talk to me, and I didn't speak to them. However, I always knew their every move, their illegal business.

One evening around midnight, Peter showed up after just finishing an internal round of the bank. He held two bottles of beer and approached me smiling.

I wondered why he came.

"Hey, dude," he said. "I thought you might need some company. So, I said to myself, why don't I see my old friend and talk about the good old days?"

I wasn't happy with this idea. I tried to remain calm, answering him as politely as I could.

"Thanks for thinking of me, but I'm working. I'm not able to hang around and chat. I have rounds to do. Sorry, you came all this way for nothing."

"Chill, man. Who will tell your boss?"

He never took anything seriously. I glanced up at the surveillance cameras so he'd understand.

Peter stared at the camera momentarily, blinked in understanding, but didn't leave. He just stepped out of range. Then he cracked open one of the beers and drank half of it in one long swig.

"There, do they see me now?" He moved even farther. "How about here?"

He acted like he was still in puberty. The anger on my face didn't sway him.

"Peter, go home. I'm working here. I can't stop for a beer while on duty. Just go home."

"No, Nikos." He glared at me. "You owe me a beer."

"Okay, fine. But not here. Not while I'm working."

"Tell me where and when then." He drank the rest of the beer, then popped the cap of the other one. "Unless you want me to come here every night."

Having already drunk his beer, he started in on the one he had brought for me.

Until he got what he wanted, he'd drive me insane. The last thing I wanted was to be seen with him.

"Okay, let's meet tomorrow at six o'clock in the afternoon in Monastiraki. By the metro. That work for you?"

He nodded, drank some of the second beer, then stepped away. "See you tomorrow. Don't stand me up, asshole, because I'll find you. We have a lot to talk about."

I wish I knew what the hell he wanted from me. I knew it was something as he couldn't have found me by chance.

The rest of the night went smoothly, and in the morning, I had the bizarre feeling that someone was following me. As much as I tried to figure it out, I couldn't be sure. Was it Peter? Someone else? One of my brother's cop friends?

I took the same path home that I always took. Then I got on the first bus I found to escape the area and got off a few stops later to hop on the right bus.

In the afternoon, I was on time outside the metro station in Monastiraki. Of course, Peter was already waiting for me. He hugged me when he saw me, which I didn't expect, patting me on the shoulder. This type of friendly gesture has always disgusted me. It makes me want to wash with alcohol. But for the sake of society, I had to be patient with others.

"At last, dude," he said. "So, what's been going on, man? What's been happening with you?"

"Let's get a few things straight between us. Just tell me what you want so we can end all this friendly discussion bullshit. I know you too well."

"Wow, man, take it easy." He raised his hands high. "I'm not chasing you. I just wanted a friendly talk with someone I used to know. How's that bad?"

I stared at him a long moment, then nodded. "Okay, we'll have that one talk. Then we move on with our lives."

He lowered his hands and nodded.

We found a quiet café in the souvenir area of Plaka, which was quite a distance from my everyday life.

"Well?" Peter started. "How have you been, Nikos?"

"I stay away from all kinds of trouble if that's what you mean. How about you?"

He shrugged. "I try as hard as I can. I don't want to go back to jail unless, of course, there's a wicked opportunity that's worth the trouble."

"What do you want? Why get involved in that shit? What's missing in your life? Is it money? Women? I don't understand why you'd take the risks. I've made my decision—I don't do that shit anymore. Nothing ever worked out right for me every time I tried to."

"Your sermon is nice. I used to have money, but now I don't."

"What happened? Did you spend it all?"

"My father, the head of the family, failed. He also made bad investments, and we all paid for it. The bank took everything he had— the villa, my father's car collection, his helicopter. Luckily, my car and an apartment in Kypseli are still mine."

"So you're looking for illegal opportunities?" I wasn't sure if he could detect the contempt in my voice.

"How will I make it without cash?"

"Work? Get a job? Like the rest of us, the humble mortals who make a living by just working every day?"

"You're crazy. I haven't worked a single day in my life. I've always been a boss, an income earner. Also, a living wage is nothing for me. I need more than a simple job could offer."

"You have a degree in anything? Secondary education?"

"Sure, I studied the art of ditching classes."

He smiled as if he'd accomplished something great. Some people have everything set up in their lives and don't appreciate it; they're not grateful.

No one gave me anything. On the contrary, they only took from me non-stop from the moment I was born. And this idiot is bragging. In any other situation, I'd have beaten the shit out of him. Instead, I put my mask on and smiled back.

"So, how have you been spending your time?"

"I've had jobs, but I've also had women who've supported me. I take care of them, especially when their husbands are gone. I get expensive gifts which I've sold." He paused and stared at me. "Don't look at me like that, like you're judging me."

"Like I'd judge you," I said, as if I was interested in his life and how he had become a fallen gigolo.

"But you thought about it. I've learned to stand out, so don't judge me."

His voice rose as if he was trying to catch everyone's attention. The waiter came to bring water and our coffee. By the expression on Peter's face, I could tell he already regretted the way he spoke.

"You know something, Nikos? You should know what kind of person you're dealing with. You can count on me, and I won't leave you behind for any reason."

"Well, as much as I understand that, I'm still not interested in any sort of criminal activity." I wasn't interested, but I'd listen to what he told me out of respect.

"My parents never married out of love. This may seem dramatic, but it defines my life even now. My mother was from a wealthy family with a large dowry, and my father carried a family name on his back, which meant a lot in society years ago. So their parents decided to marry them. They were engaged at fourteen, and they got married at eighteen. There was no love between them. How could there be when they didn't even know the real meaning of the word? Everyone had the impression that they were happy and their life was great. However, there was an issue that could not be overlooked. My father couldn't have children."

"So?"

"My mother kept my biological father a secret. When I found out, I was utterly disappointed with both my parents. My world was crushed. I felt like an outsider and did whatever I could to get kicked out of the house. They were patient with me. What else could they do? In the end, my father became a workaholic. He preferred not to see me at all. That worked well for my mother's fortune, which tripled over time, but his presence at home was non-existent. When he eventually came home, I was asleep. Other times, he didn't come home at all, and I could hear my mother crying alone. The business trips were endless as if he had another woman in his life. He tried to buy me off to avoid his guilt of not being a father. I've always had the best gifts, clothes, and a wallet full of money, which drove girls crazy and made me popular. When you have it all, you seem happy in the eyes of the world, but that doesn't mean you feel good inside. There was a time when I didn't want to see him at all, and instead of making him sad, it relieved him."

Peter paused his monologue to sip from his coffee.

"My mother has always been weak, timid, indecisive. My father took away any trace of her emotional strength. She could never do things on her own without the consent of her *master*. She looked at me passively. They let me stay in the reformatory because my father had decided it would knock some sense into me. He thought it would be best for me to change the direction of my life. The truth was that the reformatory did some good. It taught me to be smart and to organize everything without anyone catching on. I met the right people for the right things. I didn't rely on amateurs. That's how I managed to gain people's trust, and they gave me jobs. With the money women gave me, I managed to have a decent life. You can ask anyone about me. The people who know my name trust me."

"Great sermon," I echoed. "What's all this leading to?"

"I'm organizing a big hit, and your help is necessary to move forward."

Finally, he came to the reason why we were here. But why tell me his life story? To pity him?

I shook my head. "I'm sorry, my old friend. I'm out of the game."

"What? Without even listening?"

"Don't tell me." I held up my hands. "I don't even want to know."

"Come on, Nikos, you're ruining it for us. We need you. You have to join the team. Otherwise, the plan can't go forward. Everything's arranged, the schedule, the team. They're waiting for you to join start."

"I'm happy to see you, Peter." I shook my head and glanced down at the table. "But I'm done. Anyone can be replaced. I'm sure with your connections, you'll find the guy you need." I pushed back my chair and got to my feet. "See you around, man. Take care."

Continuing the meeting didn't make sense. The fact that we'd met was bad enough. I didn't like meeting someone from my past.

"Hey, sit down," Peter pleaded. "Don't leave." The bewildered look on his face made me pause.

I shook my head and stepped away. "Sorry, man, there's no need to continue. I'm out."

I walked away, having fulfilled my obligation to meet him.

I was done. Completely.

My mind racing, I went to work. I was sure that wouldn't be the last time I saw him. He'd always learned to get what he wanted. There was no way he'd give up so easily. Peter would appear sooner or later to persuade me to participate in one thing or another. Through the random act of bumping into him, he knew where I worked. There was no way he'd leave me alone now.

The rest of the night went smoothly. The bank I was protecting was a subsidiary just outside the center of Athens. No one ever approached or talked to me, not even to ask me to light a cigarette. That was exactly how I preferred it. To be left alone in my own world, to do the job required without any unexpected interruptions.

I greeted my colleague at shift change in the morning, clocked out, and headed toward the bus stop.

Peter was there.

"Good morning."

"You're not giving up, are you?" His presence pissed me off. "What didn't you understand from our conversation yesterday? I don't want to be seen with you. I have a good life and don't want to fuck that up."

"Look, Nikos, I get it, but just meet the team, get to know them, see how good they are."

"That's not going to happen. This one won't go your way." I stepped around him. "Leave me alone."

"Just relax. Let's go for a smoke." He pulled on my arm.

I followed him like an idiot as if I didn't know what kind of person he was. We stopped at a convenience store, and Peter approached the counter.

"Marlboro, please," he said to the girl behind the counter.

The second the girl turned her back, Peter put his hand in his inner pocket and withdrew a gun. I didn't have time to react. He caught me off guard.

She turned back to Peter.

"Empty the cash register, now."

The woman jumped back, staring at the weapon. "You idiot," she stammered. "They have cameras here."

Peter gestured at the till with the tip of the weapon.

The girl impressed me. She acted as if it was something she'd dealt with before. She didn't scream. She just stared at Peter as she opened the cash register.

I instantly regretted coming with him—an epic mistake.

He'd force me if he couldn't convince me to join him.

I stepped around in front of him. "What are you doing, asshole? Leave it. Let's go."

"Shut up and watch the entrance."

People had seen me with him. If there was a camera, they had me on their recording.

I had no choice. Familiar with such situations, I went to the door.

The girl was taking her time. After several moments, she handed him all the money in the till. Since the store operated twenty-four hours per day, there was also the night's cash.

"Bring me the tape from the camera," Peter said, waving the gun again.

The girl obeyed now without protest. She was extraordinary.

After giving Peter the tape, he stuffed it under his arm.

"You have to come with us," he said. "You've seen our faces."

She raised her hands. "I swear, I won't say anything. I've been robbed before. Just leave. I'll tell everyone you were wearing helmets and hoods, and I couldn't see anything. Even your accent tells me you're from abroad."

Peter shook his head. "Not happening. I can't risk it. You're coming with us. Now move." He raised the gun and aimed it at her.

"What are you doing, you asshole?" I blurted out. "Are you going to fucking take a hostage? Have you completely lost your mind? What the fuck, man?"

"Shut up, Nikos. You're acting like a saint. Hold her hands behind her back, and I'll be right behind you." He stared at the girl as she came around the counter to stand by me. "One move without being told, you'll take a bullet to the spine. Dead or disabled." Peter turned back to me. "This also applies to you, too, Nikos. I'm sorry it's come to this. I wish you'd agreed to work with me. We wouldn't have to go through this shit." He opened the door.

Everything had been pre-planned. I felt trapped, like a novice.

Peter turned the CLOSED sign, and we started walking down the street. It seemed that everyone watched us and judged us. Peter could keep the gun hidden well, though, causing no alarm.

At the car, he gave us clear instructions. The girl would sit in the back with him, and I would be the driver. As directed, I drove through side streets in the middle of nowhere.

Then, the girl began to whimper when we were clear of the downtown area.

"Shut up," Peter shouted at her.

I glanced in the rearview mirror. She cowered in the corner, trying to get away from him.

He leaned closer.

I took my eye off him to watch the road.

Then I heard a solid thump, dragging my eyes back to the mirror.

Peter had whacked the girl on the head with the end of the weapon, knocking her unconscious.

"What the fuck are you doing?" I shouted at him.

"What? You want her to see where we're going? Are you stupid?"

Something pushed my seat into my lower spine. It had to be the weapon.

"Just tell me what the fuck's going on."

"Just drive where I tell you to. I promise I'll explain everything soon enough."

I was sure the vehicle was stolen. It was old and hadn't been washed for decades. It wasn't a getaway car by any means.

When we stopped, I felt that the engine wouldn't start and would need pushing. Actually, I was hoping that would be the case. Then maybe I'd have a chance to get away from this shit.

But what about the girl?

Peter sat comfortably against the unconscious girl, staring down at her body.

His hand eased over her chest, then lowered to caress her breasts.

"Nice girl, eh? She's a little strange, but she'll do in a fix." The smile on his face widened.

I was disgusted. He'd achieved his goals, and I was his hostage. In fact, this was a first for me. As a hostage, I didn't have the upper hand; I wasn't in control of the situation, which drove me crazy.

We ended up on the outskirts of Athens, in an industrial area. We hadn't spoken to each other as I had just driven straight without further instruction.

Besides, saying anything to the asshole in the back seat wouldn't make sense. My reflexes were dulled due to a lack of sleep. My eyes were closing, too, and my courage sapped.

We stopped in a lousy neighborhood. Half of the houses were abandoned, the others left to ruin, and yet, in others, immigrants closed their windows as soon as they saw us.

They certainly didn't have proper papers because they disappeared like cockroaches when they saw me in my uniform.

"Pull over here and stop," Peter said.

I eased the car to a stop.

Peter exited the vehicle first, then opened my door.

"Let's get her out of here. Don't think about doing something crazy. No hero shit. You're already in this—all the way."

I was guilty by association as I was with him the whole time. Witnesses saw us walking together. I didn't try to stop him. Also, we shared a past since we knew each other from jail. All this combined to make me look guilty as fuck. I was so remorseful that even Kostas couldn't save me this time.

Peter whistled. A kid appeared from nowhere, and Peter gave him the surveillance tape. Everything was arranged from the beginning. This was a complete setup.

I helped him take the girl inside the house. We entered a room without windows. A yellow lamp illuminated the small space, where a dirty mattress was pushed into the corner. It reminded me of the reformatory.

We set the girl on the mattress, where he took the time to tie her before she woke, and then we went back outside. Peter locked the door behind us.

To the right of the front door was another room I hadn't seen. A couch that looked as if it had been retrieved from the city dump was up against the wall, and a board for a table sat in front of it. The house looked as if it had been built with LEGO bricks, with several additions added on later.

Moisture suffocated every breath. Even the walls seemed to be crying from the bad things that had happened inside this horrid place. Everything smelled like cigarettes and cheap cologne, and I urgently needed air. Without asking permission from Peter, I stepped outside to take a fresh breath, and he ran after me as if I was trying to escape.

"Where are you going?"

"Nowhere—to get some fresh air. How can you breathe inside that place? It fucking stinks, like something died in there."

"Come on, it's not that bad. It's all in your head." He paused momentarily, then added, "You're with me now whether you like it. You know that, right?"

Peter was so proud of his achievement.

All I could think about was the smell in that place, like a dead animal under the floorboards. My hands numbed, and a full-body sweat broke out all over me as my heart raced. I was unable to concentrate. All the germs, the larvae, the worms in the dead animal's body, and its eyes overwhelmed my thoughts.

I tried not to show my weakness, but I couldn't hide it.

"Don't panic now. You'll help us with this one job, then I'll never bother you again. I've got you on a security tape. You can't go back now. I also have the girl, and she can recognize you."

I glared at him. "What the hell are you saying? You're on the fucking tape, too, you fucking idiot."

"They don't have me. My face wasn't recorded."

I gaped at him. "How's that?" When I thought about the robbery, I realized he remained stooped over during the whole thing. At that point, everything made sense. When Peter approached me that morning, this was all planned out. He knew the store, he'd scoped it out, and he knew where the cameras were. He may have even robbed it once before to get a feeling. I couldn't rule out anything with Peter.

My breath came in short gasps, and I leaned on Peter's shoulder for balance.

"Don't freak out on me now, asshole," Peter said. "Come on, I need you."

He led me inside and made me sit on the couch, where he stuffed a joint in my mouth. Drugs were his medicine for everything.

"Take a puff to relax a little. Come on …"

Like a sheep, I obeyed him. Maybe I did need a getaway. Soon, I was in one other world—in the world of sleep-wake, which was quite familiar to me.

Images of the reformatory flashed through my mind. It haunted my soul, and I pretended to be brave and invincible, that I'd overcome everything. In all the images, Peter was beside me, fighting daily. Broken noses, jaws, blood, guards unable to tame so many wild animals.

My thoughts traveled back further. In mental pictures from the maternity hospital, I saw Katerina crying, murmuring her song. I couldn't help her. I didn't know how to help her. If I knew the cause of her pain, who had hurt her, he'd be dead, and she'd be free from her demons. In the delirium, I also saw Kiki as a young girl on her way to school before the darkness of adulthood took her; then, she was dead in a pool of blood. I took her in my arms, but she was no longer Kiki—she was Helen. She opened her eyes and stared at me, a lifeless gaze.

I woke out of breath. That was the worst thing I had ever seen—the worst part of the puzzle of my life. I was half-lying on the small couch, and Peter was there, a guard. He didn't leave me for a minute, fearing I might bolt out the door.

"Take it." He gave me a sandwich to eat. "After that, you'll feel better."

I stared at the sandwich. Did he put anything in it?

"Eat it, you asshole. I need you to be clear-headed. I still have no reason to kill you." He paused, then added, "Yet."

He was right. I wouldn't be useful to him dead. Either way, I took the risk. I looked at my watch and saw that it was three in the afternoon.

Peter leaned closer. "Call work and say you won't be coming in today. You're sick. Tell them you have food poisoning or something. You need to stay. I have to tell you the plan."

There was no way he would just let me go.

"Peter, I thought you were my friend, my mate. I don't understand why you trapped me like this."

"I did it because I know you. I need you and feel you owe me. Without me back in the reformatory, you wouldn't have survived there. Tell me, my drugs didn't make you a star player? But you forgot everything and turned your back on me. I expected more from you."

"I know you helped me, and you got paid for that. It was a mutually beneficial relationship that both of us honored, and then it was over. We weren't friends, roommates, or family, but yes, we were accomplices. I don't owe you a thing. We had an unwritten contract of limited duration. That was over years ago, and I want nothing to do with whatever you're mixed up in."

"I'm sorry you see it that way. You may have thought you were done, but not until after this deal. Then, you take the security tape and say goodbye. You go where you want."

"And the girl?"

"No one will look for her, don't worry."

"What do you mean?"

"I checked her out. She's a loner. No one will look for her."

"Okay, then tell me this magical plan of yours. It seems you've got my attention."

"I thought you'd never ask." He cleared his throat and stared at me. "We are going to rob the bank you're protecting."

My first reaction was to burst out laughing. "Come on, no way, asshole. Tell me the truth."

"That's it. That's all of it."

I gaped at him. "Are you completely crazy?"

"No, listen to me. I've thought of everything."

"I'll be arrested no matter what you think you have organized."

"Don't rush to underestimate me. I've rented the space beside your bank. Our new business will sell soil. There's a small yard at the back. Everything's legal. I have a cousin who's clean. He's started the company in his name. My team and I will be employees. We will put all the soil in bags, pack it, and take it out."

"I lost you, what soil?"

"We will dig under the bank until we get to the basement. We will create the largest tunnel ever made. The team's ready. Today, they're bringing me the bank's blueprints and building documents."

"Where will they find them?"

"You can ask him as soon as you see him."

"And the rest of the team? Who are they, and how did you find them? Are they trustworthy?"

"I will tell you the story of each one gradually, and you'll understand that I made solid choices. I can't work with him if I don't know who I'm dealing with. I need credentials. Otherwise, I don't trust people for these kinds of serious jobs. With this plan, no one will lose."

"What's my part in all this?"

"You're the reason that I had the idea in the first place. It all came together as soon as I saw that you had the night shift."

"Water," we heard the girl's voice from inside.

Peter got up and opened the door opposite me, coming out with a plastic water bottle and one straw. Then he unlocked the entrance to the room where the girl was and went inside. I thought I heard talking, but I couldn't be sure.

I got up and opened the door Peter had opened. It was a small room with a sink and a large gas stove. I turned back and paced the floor while waiting for Peter. When he exited the room with the girl, he smiled at me and then winked.

"And when we get bored, we'll have someone to entertain us." He gestured at the room.

I wanted to throw up. I hated guys like Peter, guys who destroy girls like Kiki.

"Peter, I'm going home. I need a shower."

"I don't think so."

"Peter, there's no way I will do or say anything. You hold all the cards—you won. Maybe I owe you something, but I don't have a leash. I never have a leash. If you want me on the team, these are my terms. I don't even like the fucking cops." I had to leave this place. I couldn't stand spending another minute there.

"Okay, I understand what you're saying, but you must be here anyway to meet someone."

"Then I'll be back." I moved toward the door. "I need to get some fresh air."

"I'm sorry, Nikos, you're right. I'll guide you to the main road to orient yourself. You'll figure out how to take the bus from there. At nine o'clock, the other person comes. Arrange to be here. If you're not here, any trust we have between us will dissolve."

I nodded. "At least tell me who this person is."

"You'll see."

Peter moved outside, and I followed him. Without another word, we got back in the car. For over ten minutes, he explained how to arrive back at the house. He'd made sure to find the most isolated place.

He left me on the street by a bus stop filled with people who had finished their shifts at the refineries and shipyards and were headed home. People sacrificed their lives and youth in the name of an honest living. I could never be like that. Maybe for a short time with the right mask, but not for long—I would explode.

I entered the bus along with these people. The air on the bus was suffocating, full of sweat, bad breath, and germs. Dressed in the security uniform, it felt like all eyes were on me. I still wasn't used to that.

I rode that bus home, locked in my own tired mind.

How far would I take this? Would I actually go through with the robbery of the bank that hired me to protect it?

Or should I just come back tonight and kill Peter?

I fell asleep on the bus thinking about a dead Peter.

Chapter 15

When I managed to get back home, I went directly to my room.

Kostas was home, so I avoided him.

I removed my uniform, showered, and scrubbed off the germs—their breaths, sweat, smoke, stench, and looks. As the water fell on me, I thought of the girl locked in that room. Her gaze had seemed empty, like she had no life, nothing to live for. Who could know what had happened in her life before she was unlucky enough to meet us? How can someone save or destroy another person's life in a single moment? It only takes a moment, a mistake, a crime, a car accident, a bullet—how could this be possible?

I never abused women. I may have used them but never abused them. After reading Kiki's diary, I saw things in a different light. Unless someone came at me and disrespected me, I left others alone now. I didn't want to bother anyone. I didn't want to fight.

Although, my point of view was vastly different from most. If I was involved in a fight, I imagined myself beating the other guy mercilessly until his last breath wheezed out. Since justice never comes, why would mercy show up? I wanted to vent my intense anger on anyone who was a bully and was messing with others so many times, but I held back. I would end up in jail or a psychiatric ward somewhere, and I would disappoint the only one I still had in my life, Kostas.

When I was about to leave the apartment, Kostas was waiting for me in the living room.

"Don't you have a shift today?"

"I got a day off."

"You're lying."

"What I need the least right now is an interrogation. This is our home, not the police station, and I'm not your prisoner."

"I got a call from your boss."

"And?"

"They asked when you would feel well enough to return to work. He said something about arranging the schedule. What was I supposed to say?"

"Just stay out of my life, and we'll be fine."

"I know you. I only need to look you in the eye to understand something's going on."

"Something's going on, eh Kostas? Look, I'm in no mood for your theories right now. Do whatever you want with your life, and leave me alone." I slammed the door.

I was almost sure Kostas wouldn't stay put. When he suspected me of wrongdoing, he would tell his cop buddies to watch me.

This meant I had to watch my ass.

It took me a long time to find Peter's house. I got lost several times on the road while trying to figure out how I could get rid of this trap Peter had pulled me into. But no matter how hard I thought about it, I couldn't find a way out. He had sucked me in good, and now I was caught in that store's camera lens. If I killed Peter, the kid who had the tape would deliver it to the police, and I would be charged with more crimes than one.

And what about the girl? I couldn't leave her behind. If I left her, I would hear in the news that a body was found in the ditch somewhere. She would have been raped and murdered without her head or fingerprints. No one would look for her, and they would bury her as a Jane Doe.

However, I concluded that it would be easier for me to kill everyone to escape the situation. Only the girl troubled me. In her face, I saw Kiki, I saw Helen.

The only thing that helped me find Peter's place was the parked car we'd used earlier. The front door was closed but not locked—completely careless.

I pushed it open and stepped inside, then went directly to the room where the girl was being held and opened that door.

Peter was on top of her. The girl wasn't making a sound.

I closed the room door and moved into the living room full of rage, a rage I tried to suppress. Otherwise, I'd just murder everyone and fuck the consequences.

Peter came out after a while, buttoning his pants.

"Come on," he said. "It's your turn. She's ready. She's a good little whore, quiet, and doesn't resist much." He nodded toward the door. "Go ahead." His tone was one of pride like he'd *taken* his woman.

I knew how these things worked. Fucking her made me an accomplice. *Not* fucking her meant I couldn't be trusted that I wouldn't be part of the team.

"Okay, I'll go, but I don't want an audience." I gave him a warning glare.

"Okay, buddy, whatever you say." Peter dropped onto the sofa and lit a cigarette.

I got the key, unlocked the door, stepped inside, then locked it again. The girl was gathered on the edge of the mattress up against the wall.

"Please," she whispered.

I could hardly hear her. I edged close and stroked her cheek. She pulled away gently from me. At that moment, from the subdued look in her eye, she understood that I had the power and the strength to do anything I wanted for her. But did I have the right?

"Don't be afraid," I whispered. "I've done many crazy things in my life, but I never was, and I'll never be, a rapist." I paused a moment to let that sink in. "I'm not going to hurt you in any way, I promise."

She stared at me, fear evident in her eyes.

"Nevertheless, I want something from you."

"What?" she managed to say, her eyes wide in expectation of what I wanted.

"I need you to moan like we're having sex. I need them to think I'm on their side." I whispered in case Peter was listening by the door.

She tried to smile, but instead, it turned into a grimace. A tear had dropped to the side of her lips. I took in the other side of her face, which she had been lying on, and her eye was swollen. Peter must have slapped her hard or punched her. This angered me at levels I'd never felt before. I couldn't make these marks disappear, but I could do something about it so it would never happen again.

"What's your name?" I said in a low tone as I sat down next to her.

"Lisa."

"Why would you work in that stupid store? So many bad things happen in that area. You knew it wasn't safe enough."

"It's a long story," she said, her voice hoarse.

"We have time. We're supposed to be fucking."

"I come from the classic reformatories, damaged parents, drugs. I soon realized I'd always be living in this shit." She lowered her gaze as if she would find an answer on the floor. From the posture of her body, I saw she didn't want to talk anymore. I didn't insist on further discussion.

As she was curled up on the mattress, I saw the words "Never

Forget" tattooed on her wrist. Wrapped around the letters was a snake, its mouth open. I wondered what it was that she didn't want to forget. Why tattoo it on her wrist?

I sat there for about fifteen minutes in silence. She made a few moans, and then I got up, unlocked the door, and stepped out into the other room.

"Did you feed her?" I asked Peter. "She's listless."

"Yeah, man."

"And did she eat?"

"No."

"You know something, Peter? I will do whatever you want, without tapes and bullshit, but I want her to be mine."

"Nah." He shook his head. "Since when did you soften? Since when do whores have value?"

"I didn't soften." I acted put out, pissed off. "I want her for my personal needs. No one touches her, not even you. Do we have a deal?"

Peter didn't answer immediately. He slowly and irritably lit another cigarette, puffed several times, then eased back on the couch.

"Even though I have no fucking idea what you want to gain from it, I promise I won't touch her again. As for the others, I can't guarantee shit. If they agree, then you won't have a problem. So, congratulations on having a new dog. You can water it, feed it, but you can't let it out for a walk."

He actually thought he was being smart.

This move I made put me in jeopardy. Who knew what kind of men Peter would have found to help with the job? It was the first time in my life I felt my conscience. The first time, I considered protecting someone I barely knew.

Part of the reason was that I had begun to *feel*. After Helen's death, I discovered what it was like to feel something. Love, kindness, remorse. With Helen, I felt like I had pulled the trigger. Even Mrs. Cleo's dead face with the bullet between her eyes no longer comforts me.

Maybe with the girl in the other room, I might be redeemed and feel better about what I had done and where I'd come from. If I saved her, perhaps I would make up for not saving Katerina, Helen, or Kiki. If I had read her diary earlier, maybe things would be different.

"Peter, just tell others that the girl was a mistake in the plan. A mistake that I'm going to fix. Cool?"

"I don't make mistakes in my plans, so I can't say anything like that. You can tell them yourself that you'll be the only one taking care of her from here on in."

"Yes, but what about when I'm not here at night? You'll be able to take care of her without touching her?"

"I'll do my best." He met my gaze, his eyes narrowed. "When did you become so soft?"

"I have my fucking reasons." I stepped to the window, then back to the couch, pacing the room.

"One of the team will be here soon. I warn you, though, he's weird. He's done a whole series of robberies and murders."

I shrugged as I paced. "Like all of us."

"No, trust me. He doesn't have any moral barriers. He has no perception of right and wrong. There is only one way, and it's his way."

"Aren't we all like that?" Was he trying to scare me? If so, he was wasting his time. Nobody scared me, not even death itself.

"I should tell you a bit about him before he comes so you'll know who you're dealing with."

Peter went on to tell me that Stavros was about our age. His parents were teenagers when they had him. His mother was a foreigner, and his father was cruel and ignorant. They fed him and thought that would be enough. His parents fought so often, especially when he became a teenager. Stavros saw the world differently. He saw it as hostile, dark. He got involved with gangs and skipped school.

Once the police arrested him for petty crimes, he ended up in the reformatory for six months. That's where he associated more with the underworld. After they let him out, he was arrested again. He could never adjust to school or any job.

He came of age and had to go to the army. No one can avoid the Greek army. Yet, he couldn't tame his kleptomania. Although he tried to adapt, it was impossible to operate within a discipline.

At one point, he was accused of theft inside and outside the camp. He did what he could to avoid arrest, but it was impossible. His lousy behavior, plus the thefts, sent him to a military prison.

At that time, in addition to being a fugitive, he was also declared a deserter. For a year, he kept a low profile. Tried to stay away from trouble but couldn't hide for long. During an armed robbery, the police arrived and chased him. In order to escape, Stavros shot randomly at them several times, missing every single time. They caught him, and he went back to prison again, where he met others like him. Upon his release, he continued where he left off, but not alone this time. He had company.

They robbed hotels and travel agencies in Athens for two months without the police arresting them. During one robbery, they weren't careful enough, and it cost the life of one of his partners. He couldn't handle it, so he called a TV program and threatened that after the cops killed one of his, he would kill three. But the cops were smarter and ended up arresting him again, even though he was armed. That same day, another partner was killed by the cops.

"That would make him furious." I'd stopped pacing and was sitting on the floor listening now.

Peter nodded. "At that point, he couldn't do much. After another year in prison, he tried to escape. Stavros couldn't stand imprisonment. At this point, he's the most famous, most well-known among us."

"Why have someone like that on the team? If anyone recognizes him, it'll ruin our plans."

"Don't worry. He'll wear a disguise."

"I don't know. This guy has shot at cops. They'll hunt him down without mercy."

Peter shook his head. "It isn't that easy to get him. Once when he realized the cops had located him, he escaped again. He has stolen from bakeries, pharmacies, and many others. Best of all, he robbed a bank once. They tried to catch him again, organizing a massive operation. More than one hundred police officers on the surrounding streets and a bunch more in his apartment waited for him. Stavros got away with only one bullet in his leg."

"Remind me why we need him?"

"He has a lot of experience in robberies and knows how to stay hidden from cops. Imagine all the years the cops have been chasing him. He gets away every time. It's like a movie."

"Maybe you're right. However, I don't know how we'll all bond."

"Why would you say that? We'll be fine."

"How much money do you think we'll make?"

"Look, I've watched the vehicles unload money there. The building's old. I can't know what work they've done in the basement, though. I expect to have the building's plans that were submitted to the government soon."

"How accurate will they be? I mean, do they actually have the bank's plans in a common public office?"

"Look, we have the time to think over the details. The most important thing is to make our way in. All the digging will be done at night. During the day, we'll get rid of the soil. I need you to be on the night shift so you won't try to deal with us. You must watch out the entrance and not let anyone bother us."

"It isn't that easy. I have to make rounds and check three specific places. I have a key and put in the particular lock so my bosses can see when I was there."

"We can arrange the time based on your schedule."

I had a bad feeling about all of this, and in the end, I was so right.

I should've listened to my gut and walked away.

I'm sure my life would've turned out so much better if I had.

Chapter 16

We sat and watched TV for almost an hour before there was a knock on the door. Peter got up and opened it. A tall, unshaven guy with long black hair and glasses stepped inside. He didn't sit. He just stood there, scrutinizing the room.

Peter patted the couch. "Come on, Stavros, sit down." He pointed at me. "That's the guy I was telling you about."

"Did he accept?" His eyes roved over me from head to toe.

"He accepted, but I had to convince him some. Also, I've got a girl inside." Peter pointed at the room where the girl was being held captive.

Stavros nodded, then sat across from me, his eyes fixed on me the whole time. He tried to intimidate me and show me he was the boss. I didn't care one bit. No amount of bravado would beat a slit throat, which is what he would have if he overstepped. I had met other guys like him. He wasn't the first one, nor would he be the last.

I looked at him just as intensely. Peter fidgeted like he was feeling awkward. From the corner of my eye, I saw Peter scratching his head.

"Did he tell you?" Stavros asked.

"Yes."

"And?"

"Nothing."

"If you betray me, I will kill you. I keep my word."

"I'm not betraying anyone."

"Peter said you're okay."

"I am."

"Fine." He relaxed on the couch, removed his glasses and the wig, and scratched his shaved head.

The more I looked at him, the more I realized I had seen him before. All the failed police efforts had been discussed in the media. His last escape saw several resignations at the police station.

"Do you believe in this bank job?" I asked.

"If I didn't, why would I risk it? I want one last job, then I'll disappear. Having the authorities on my ass for so long has me tired."

"I can relate to that."

He nodded. "Yes, I understand your help will be important to the success of this job."

"I have one condition, though. No one touches the girl in there. She's mine. And when this is done, she leaves with me."

"I don't care about the girl. In fact, I don't want her to see me. I aim to limit my exposure to witnesses while participating in this job." He shrugged. "I never leave witnesses behind. So make sure she doesn't see me."

"Understood," I replied evenly.

Stavros took a small bag from his pocket, went to the kitchen, and returned refreshed.

"Cocaine, you bitch," he muttered to himself. "You've taken all my money." He studied the wall for a moment in a vacant stare.

"How many people will we be?" I asked Peter.

"The less you know, the better for you. What's important for now is you to go back to work and drop to the lowest floor."

"It has no lower floor."

"It sure does. Maybe it's stuffy, or perhaps it's covered in wood, but it's there. You have to search and tell me what you find out. I've seen the plans for the original building, so I know there was a basement there."

"Where are the plans?"

"The less you know, the better. I'll tell you when the time comes."

"Okay. When will I meet the others? Before I fully commit to this job, I need to know my team. I know you, Peter, but since I'm risking my head, I need to know everyone. We're already complicit in the hostage situation."

"Stavros will stay here to watch the girl, and we will go and find the others. It's not easy for them to move."

"Why are they disabled?"

"No, they're fugitives."

Fugitives? What the fuck?

"Okay, let's go," I said, tired of discussing this shit.

We left Stavros behind to stare at the wall. All I hoped was that he wouldn't touch the girl. I had seen what could happen to a woman in a man's hands, and I didn't want to see her like that.

I got in the old car, and Peter dropped in the driver's seat. We embarked on a long journey through the countryside. We passed the signs of small towns in the dark. I didn't ask where we were going since I already knew the answer. This secrecy was getting on my nerves. I wasn't used to being someone's puppet.

As he drove, I thought about grabbing him by the neck and choking the life out of him. But I knew that either death or prison awaited me if I tried. I had to ensure I was clear of this shit first, then kill the bastard. Based on what Peter did to that girl, the man Peter had become, I knew that before this was over, I would kill my old friend.

We drove most of the night and finally arrived in the mountains. We left the car at one point on the road, one only farmers used, and then started walking uphill. The whole night, Peter drove silently, and I fought to stay awake, thinking about killing Peter.

On the mountain, everything seemed different. I had never been so close to nature. I was the child of the system, the city. I took deep breaths as we passed through the trees.

"Do you know where we're going?" I asked, and then the idea came to me that he was taking me somewhere remote to kill me.

"Don't worry. I've been here before. I know my way. We're here to find two brothers. They're professionals, Dimitris and George. The older one, Dimitris, started his career at nineteen with robberies and burglaries. The younger one, George, didn't follow him immediately. Later on, Dimitris convinced his brother to join him, and now they're joining us."

Peter told me these brothers went from city to city and stole from jewelry stores. They worked a system and were doing well for themselves. Then, they added another to their group.

When Dimitris got arrested, George couldn't abandon his brother. He threw a rope over the prison wall and got him out, then the brothers disappeared.

After this embarrassing escape, the cops searched all of Greece to find George, but they couldn't catch the brothers.

Soon, jewelry stores weren't enough for them. They wanted something more challenging, so they robbed the National Bank. During their escape, as cops chased them on foot, they threw thousands of drachmas on the road. The public went wild, obscuring the officers' ability to continue the chase.

"Geez, what kind of guys are these?"

"It doesn't stop there. They robbed more banks, kidnapped someone, and got more money."

"So much money." I shook my head. "What are they doing with all that cash?"

"No one knows, but my acquaintances at the police station say they've invested most of it abroad."

"What have they been up to since? Did they stop, slow down, or remain in hiding?"

"As luck would have it, the younger brother was involved in a traffic accident, and they caught him again. The older brother organized another prison break—Hollywood bullshit. He forced a helicopter pilot to land in the prison yard. His brother and another inmate boarded, leaving the authorities speechless. No one expected them to be capable of such a thing."

"And after?"

"I reached out to them for this robbery through a friend. I told them about the plan, and they were thrilled as they had never done anything like this before."

"And you're sure they aren't being monitored by the cops in any way?"

Peter shook his head. "No such surveillance that I'm aware of. Also, they're not murderers, just thieves."

They seemed too good to be true, so I stopped asking questions. Peter praised the team he'd put together. I had my reservations and was sure that at some point, everyone would want to do their own thing, to work autonomously. When you learn to rely on yourself, being a member and not a leader is difficult. I wondered how some of them accepted this gig after all. It couldn't be so simple. What was going through my mind was that maybe they had information about underground bars of gold. Something so big that they'd kill the others to keep for themselves once we were inside.

We had climbed a huge hill covered with fir trees and the odor of the earth. After an hour, we came upon a hut.

Peter whistled a familiar tune. "If I hadn't whistled, we would've been shot where we stand."

"I thought you said these guys weren't murderers."

Peter smiled and opened his mouth to say something, but the door opened.

A middle-aged man with a small protruding belly stepped outside.

"Welcome, guys," he said with a smile.

"I'm Dimitris, and this is George." He pointed behind him.

Another middle-aged man, with darker hair and medium height stepped into view. Visually, they were nothing like the notorious robbers Peter described. They looked more like poor farmers.

Their hut had bare necessities. Two beds, a fireplace, one tiny kitchen, and a bathroom. The walls were decorated with family photos, although they weren't in a single photo.

"We're here to take you with us," Peter said. "Now that we have our Nikos on our team." He gestured at me like we were in a TV game show. "The plan begins."

They both glared at me with distrust in their eyes.

"We're not going back to prison," George said, staring at me. "Prepare to play your role well."

"I'm not the one to worry about," I replied, speaking the truth. Peter was the weakest link, and then Stavros was back at the house.

I leaned against the wall by the door and waited for them to prepare. They wiped the place down, collected their backpacks, and closed the door behind them. It was as if they had done it a thousand times before.

They both wore sunglasses, fake beards, and wigs, making them appear as if they'd escaped from some 1980s movie. After the long hike down the hill, they took the back seat, with Peter behind the wheel. The smell of their breath, cigarettes and alcohol, was unbearable.

"Well, Nikos," Dimitris whispered behind me, "you aren't too talkative, are you?"

"I have nothing to say. I'm sure Peter has filled you in on me. I trust he hasn't missed anything."

"True, but he did leave one small detail aside."

"Okay, shoot." I twisted in the seat to look back at the brothers. "What is it you want to know?"

"How'd you get out of the reformatory all those years ago?"

"They let me out due to good behavior."

Dimitris smiled and crossed his arms over his ample belly. "Tell us the truth."

"That is the truth." I twisted back around to stare out the windshield. "Check into it if you don't believe me, but isn't that a little late now?" I was sure they wouldn't believe my lie, but no one questioned me further. Of course, I could've also asked them why they were endangering their freedom and why with Peter and Stavros. But I preferred silence over checking into them.

On our way back, we stopped for gas, but that was it. Peter knew all the regional roads, and that's why it took us so long. He couldn't risk falling into a blockade. All the way, they were talking about the most irrelevant things. They debated the best singer and how to cook a steak. It was as if we were on a relaxed excursion without a care in the world.

If we were animals, we would be tigers, and the cage would be our car. At any critical moment, one of us could easily eat the flesh of the other—we all knew and felt the danger of the other.

Peter left me at the train station so I could go home to change. I hadn't slept a minute as I remained on guard, watching my back, which exhausted me further.

As was usual, Kostas was waiting for me in the living room.

"Why are you here?" I asked him. "Are you sick, or did you leave work early?"

"I just wanted to hang out with my brother for a while," he said, trying to play it cool.

I knew him better than that. "I'm going to shower and then get some sleep because yesterday I had a crazy night, and I haven't closed my eyes."

"I know you haven't slept here." He moved closer to me. "When you get involved with that shit you used to do, I can smell it on you. Where were you, and who were you with?"

"Who's asking? My brother, my dad, or a detective?"

"Nikos, I know you well. Don't change the subject."

I moved toward the bathroom. "I want to go to sleep. Leave me alone."

"I will tell you one thing. If you're stuck in this shit again, whatever you're involved in, I won't be there to save you. My career won't last another family scandal involving you."

"Don't worry about shit like that. Nothing's happening."

I had no choice. Nor could I do anything. I felt trapped. I didn't want to be involved in all this. How could I explain that to him? It would only make the situation worse. If I gave him any information, he would feel obligated to intervene and report it to his colleagues. If he didn't, he would be an accessory, an accomplice, or whatever they called it. So, to continue with Peter's crew, I had to keep my brother in the dark.

Ultimately, I saw it as saving my brother's life and career.

While ending mine.

Chapter 17

I SHOWERED, SLEPT DEEPLY, and then dressed to go to my job. Peter's job would start tonight, and I had to be ready to play it right. I arrived to work on time, as always.

When I met up with my coworker, he seemed worried about me.

"You look like shit," he said. "What happened to you?"

"I ate something that was off." I touched my stomach. "And it bothered me. But I'm better now." I patted him on the back and left. After checking in, I did my rounds as I was supposed to. Around midnight, a truck marked Earthworks parked next door.

I moved to the window to watch as the gang opened the store and disappeared inside. I had no idea what they were doing there for so long, but after a while, they came out and unloaded the truck. They had packed everything in large wooden boxes. Nothing was visible, nothing left to chance.

Then I did another round. I toured the entire bank before heading to the basement. I wondered how they'd manage to dig and come up at the right place. Maybe Peter's friend, the one with the bank's blueprints, worked inside the bank. That had to be it. Or he worked at City Hall.

When I returned upstairs and moved to the side window, the truck was still parked next door.

That night seemed endless. My eyelids wanted to close, but I had a job to do. I was there to protect the bank until they robbed it.

I stepped outside to do a perimeter check when a streetwalker approached me. She was a regular in this area, but we never spoke. She had caked on her makeup but was barely dressed. She held a cigarette and stared at me.

"What happened? You don't look good today."

"I work late hours. Not much I can do."

"You want a drink?"

I shook my head. "I'm working. Just leave."

"You know everyone's wondering about that huge truck. Why's it parked there in the middle of the night? Some of the girls saw a bunch of these weird guys going inside that store."

"Why would I know about a truck not on the bank's property?"

She shrugged. "Who knows? You're the guy in the uniform."

"My interests are the security of the bank and nothing else. I'm not a cop. I'm not a savior. Now, head back to your corner."

"Okay, don't bite my head off." She strode away, swinging her hips, leaving the scent of her cheap perfume behind.

The fact that the truck was noticed and being discussed was a problem. That there was interest in it was a problem.

I watched her sashay back to her pimp—the guy with the shaved head.

Morning came, and everything seemed the same. No one had left the store beside the bank. I was so curious to find out what they were doing, but I couldn't go and check on them.

The girl back at Peter's house came to mind. I wondered who was with her, taking care of her. I went home, showered, and left for Peter's house. Fortunately, Kostas wasn't home, so I didn't have to report to him about my movements.

I had the feeling that people on the bus were watching me. If Kostas had put a tail on me, he would complicate my life more than I could imagine. Eventually, my fatigue betrayed me, and I fell asleep in the bus seat until the bus reached its final destination.

"Dude, wake up." The bus driver's voice came through to me.

It was so hard to open my eyes. I was beyond tired, and my body felt like I'd been beaten.

I stepped off the bus in a daze and had to walk back as I'd missed several stops. At the house, the door was half open. I entered slowly, not knowing what danger I might face behind the door.

Stavros was stoned out of his head, sleeping on the couch. Without making any noise, I took the keys from the table and opened the door to check on the girl.

I approached and sat next to her. At first, I thought she was sleeping, but she wasn't. There was a syringe next to her on the floor. Stavros did that. I returned to the living room without much thought and slapped him awake. Who knows what happened when I was away?

He was so stoned that he couldn't wake up, so there was no point hitting him. But that didn't mean that I wouldn't confront him later. I returned to the room and sat across from the girl, where I inadvertently fell asleep.

In my troubled sleep, there were many images of what had happened to me recently. Peter was there. But what scared me was how I saw the girl in front of me transforming into Helen and then becoming herself again, blood running from her mouth and her eyes wide, crystal clear, lifeless.

When I opened my eyes, she was sleeping as I had left her. I realized I was tied to her fate. Peter had taken care of that. I wouldn't let anything happen to her. I couldn't bear the fact that Helen took a bullet for me. It would've hit me if I were so lucky and ended my parasitic, monotonous life.

I went to her and caressed her hand. She couldn't feel a thing. The more I looked at her, the more I wanted to know her story. She didn't look innocent or naïve. I would learn, though, as it was only a matter of time.

In the other room, Stavros was still sleeping on the couch. I wanted to kill him, even though he hadn't done anything bad. Just seeing him pissed me off. He was definitely on my murder list. I got a bucket of water and emptied it on his head. When he realized what had happened, I would already be gone. I needed to get to work and check on the others.

The truck was still parked outside the store. I did my patrols the way I normally would. I scanned everything and peered everywhere, although I would like to have eyes in the back of my head, too. Also, I needed to slip out of Peter's supervision to take a day off and catch up on sleep.

The truth was that there were noises from the building next door, and I had to cover them. They had started digging. Maybe they'd brought a drill. They deliberately had me on the outside of the plan. The more I thought about it, the angrier I became. As I fumed, I had an idea of their plan. They would do the job, kill the girl, and load everything on me. It would be so fucking easy for them to plant the evidence in the bank after they leave. I was the ideal victim. I had to find a way to get things twisted around in my favor. There was no way I would go to jail because of them. I couldn't stand going to jail.

The night passed slowly, and I felt ready to explode. Something had to be done.

In the morning, after greeting my colleague, I went home quickly. I needed sleep to think clearly. I phoned work and asked for a day off. The supervisor asked me if I was well, but then he agreed. It was the second day off in months.

I took a warm bath, shaved, and stared at myself in the mirror. I looked about sixty years old—although I was in my mid-thirties—as if I didn't have a trace of life inside me, and maybe that was true. As soon as I came out of the bathroom, Kostas was there. He scared the crap out of me.

"Why do you look like shit?" he asked.

"The night shifts are beating me up."

"Did you start up some shit again?"

"Did you start the interrogation again? We can't even have a normal conversation without you turning it into an interrogation."

"Shut up. I'm talking to you like a brother. I worry about you when I see you looking like this."

"Don't make me regret coming home."

"Yes, of course, I'm bothering you."

"Of course, you're bothering me. You're always so perfect, so good. The good brother, the good son, the good student, the good cop. So much perfection becomes exhausting, dude. Let me stay in my misery and imperfection. I'm not like you and will never be like you." I didn't want to hear any more of his shit.

Kostas stared at me in amazement. "What are you saying? Do you even listen to what you're saying? What would you do if you were in my position?"

"Who told you I wanted you to be in that position?"

"No one, but I had to take on that responsibility since you were always so problematic."

"Problematic? After all the shit we went through, you, of all people, could say that I'm problematic?"

"We went through the same shit. But you chose to live the way you do. We had common ground, a common starting point."

"You're wrong. There's nothing common about us."

"Then tell me, why don't you want to be a good person?"

"Because you had already taken that place. I have to be something else."

"You could be better."

"No, I couldn't, and I can't. I am the inappropriate, the dirty, the corrupted, the hated."

"What the fuck are you saying? Why do you tell this shit to yourself? Who hates you?"

"Why don't you ask me who likes me instead?"

"When you don't love yourself, how do you expect others to?" Those were his last words. I slammed my door as I left. I honestly didn't want to hear anything else. I took a sedative, and after a while, I slept soundly, without dreams, as if I'd died. In fact, I wish I'd died.

I woke at dawn, got dressed quickly, and left. I wanted to find the guy with the shaved head and knew where to look. He organized groups of girls in five places. Every night, he checked on everything and stopped at a strip club in Syggrou Avenue. I was sure I'd find him there.

At the club, the girls were all there. One guy stood outside the door, staring at me. I didn't pay him much attention. I waited for my turn and went inside. He stepped in front of me.

"Reservation?"

"Since when?"

"Name?"

"Dinos."

"Well, Dino, have you made a reservation?"

"I don't need one. Call your boss."

He frowned and stepped aside. He seemed funny to me, like a monkey wearing a suit. In the background, there was a second door where a blonde stood like a statue, her pert silicone breasts on display.

"Come on." She took me by the hand and led me inside.

Someone with my history would think I was in my natural place. But no, I hated every square inch of this place. The men who ogled the naked dancers disgusted me. They were whores as well, their hands full of germs after touching the dancers everywhere. There were certainly diseases here. With all these germs, there was no escape.

The bar area was full of men, but the pimp wasn't there. One of his men was, though. He held a drink in his hand, a cigarette in the other He crushed the butt in an ashtray, then scanned the strip club.

His eyes locked on me. Although the place was dark, I could feel it. When there's darkness inside you, we recognize each other as if we have a mark on our forehead.

He waved me over, and I approached. This man wanted to show me how important he was. I knew guys like him.

"Where's your boss?" I asked, loud enough to be heard over the thumping bass.

"I'm the boss."

I laughed. "No, you're not. I need to speak with your boss."

He nodded to another monkey in the background, who stepped closer and then accompanied me to the end of the bar, where we stopped at the door. He knocked twice, then opened it. The boss sat in the office; a gun sat in plain sight on top of his desk. The rest of the room was covered in an old beige wallpaper, stained gray from years of cigarette smoke. The air was so thick with weed smoke that anyone who entered this room left happy.

"What does a fucking cop want with me?" he asked, placing a hand on his jacket. He had to have another gun hidden there.

"Chill, I'm not a cop. I'm a security guard at the bank—big difference." I moved closer. "I need a favor." I gestured at the chair.

After a moment, he nodded, and I took a seat.

"What can I do for you? Or better yet, what can you do for me?"

"I'm looking for information about a girl."

"One of my girls?"

"I'm not sure. Don't you know all the girls wandering around the center?"

"Perhaps. What does she look like?"

"Her head is shaved on one side, black hair on the other side. Big green eyes, thin and lean." I met his gaze, but he didn't blink. The man was emotionless.

"What are you going to do for me?"

"First, just tell me if you know her or not."

"No, all negotiations go my way, or there isn't a negotiation."

"Then tell me what you want."

"I want to know who those guys are moving into my territory next to the bank. Some of my boys say they are well-known."

Shit. Peter's plan was falling apart, and he didn't know it.

"What do you care?" I asked.

He smiled as he studied me. "I'll amuse you with an answer, but that's not part of our negotiation." He leaned forward, taking his hand off his jacket and resting on his elbows. "I don't need other guys in my territory, especially the kind of men I suspect are in that building. If the police come and poke their noses into my business, there'll be hell to pay."

"As far as I know, they're opening a company that'll sell soil to landscaping companies or some shit. Now, what about the girl?"

"You don't want to know." An ugly smirk crossed his face.

"Tell me about her." My fists clenched, and I got out of my seat. I didn't like people fucking with me.

The bald guy put his hand on the gun. "What do you care about some chick?"

"She has something that belongs to me."

"Tell me again about the guys selling soil. Tell me what you know, and I'll tell you about the girl."

"Fuck it."

I left the strip club struggling with my thoughts. I wanted to know about the girl but couldn't expose the job. I couldn't tell that pimp who was actually in the building next door to the bank.

But I needed to learn what the gang was doing. So I made my way back to the bank and strode to the store's front door. I knew where my colleague would be inside the bank, so I wasn't worried I'd be seen. I knocked on the door three times, then waited.

Stavros opened the door, grabbed me by the collar, and dragged me inside.

"What are you doing here? Do you want to ruin everything? And what the hell was wrong with you yesterday?"

"We'll discuss that another time."

"No, we'll talk now." He was so agitated his eyes bulged.

I moved into position to fight him when Peter came in from another room.

"Are you crazy?" he shouted. "What're you doing here, and who's in your position?"

"I'm covered at the bank."

Peter stepped in front of me. "Fine, but what are you doing here?"

"I'm in all the way, or I'm out. I want to know what you guys are doing."

"Sorry, you're right." Peter took me by the shoulder. It was clear he didn't want any tension. He led me to another room and asked Stavros to guard the door. He closed the door behind him, and I turned to see Dimitris in front of me, covered in dust. They had already dug the hole, and each man had to use a ladder to go down into it. There were packed bags with soil, and they had even arranged to add a sticker with their logo. I went down the ladder and found they had built a small tunnel. Peter followed me and let Dimitris go to have a cigarette and rest.

"Is the other one with the girl?"

"Yes, since you're supposed to be in your post." He glared at me. "What you did today, never do it again. You put us all in danger. Fortunately, we didn't use the drill yet. We had to talk first."

"Okay, how do I get my share? Where exactly will I find you?"

"I'll let you know. We still have a few days to work. Will you be able to keep yourself together until we're finished?"

"Yes."

"Look at me. We're not playing here. That shit you pulled with Stavros"—he shook his head—"I won't be able to protect you. And what the fuck is it about that chick, anyway. Do you know her from before, or do you have some sort of prior connection? I mean, dude, you just met her, and you're doing all this shit."

"Stavros gave her drugs."

"And what do you care?"

"We agreed."

"Okay, I'll tell him she's your toy. But if she gets in the way, she's dead."

Dimitris interrupted our discussion.

"He's here."

"Let's go upstairs. I'll introduce you to our last member."

We went back up to the main floor. Another partner?

"Kyriakos, let me introduce you to Nikos," Peter said.

The man in front of me had black eyebrows and curly hair. He seemed ordinary, but I could see a darkness in his eyes.

There was a strange silence until it became apparent that they wanted to talk, and I was in the way. Peter didn't tell me there would be another guy on the team. They hid that from me, and I was sure they were hiding more.

"Can you watch the door so Dimitris can leave since we can't use the drill tonight?"

"Sure," I said, and I left the building. I wanted to check on the girl anyway. I took Peter's old car and left in the middle of the night. When I got to the house, I entered using the key on Peter's ring, then opened the inside door gently to see what the girl was doing. I turned on the hall light to see better without waking her. I didn't like what I saw at all. She was curled up, hugging her legs tight and shaking rhythmically, back and forth.

"Tell me what happened," I said.

Her response was a murmured melody. This melody was so familiar to me that my heart beat wildly. Pictures from the maternity hospital flooded my mind. Was it even possible?

"Katerina?" I whispered.

The girl raised her head, and I saw her swollen face. She had been beaten up, and who knew what else had happened to her while I was away.

"How do you know …" she stammered, "Katerina?"

"Tell me, are you Katerina?" I gripped her wrist to keep her focused on me.

"Katerina, who?"

"Just answer me." My hand tightened more than I intended, and she pulled away.

"There was a girl named Katerina. My roommate years ago. She decided to change her life and move on. Nevertheless, there are hundreds of Katerinas out there."

"If this Katerina, the one you lived with, had ever been to a maternity hospital, then she's the one I knew."

"She never told me about her past." Her eyes fixed on mine. "Why did you call me Katerina?"

"I met her in that hospital. When something terrible happened to her, she never discussed it. She would just curl up, shake, and mutter the melody you were humming."

The girl's mouth dropped open. Then she winced as it caused her pain. "I've seen my Katerina do that. She said something about collecting pieces of her soul. It was her way of gaining strength while maintaining sanity. I tried that in my life, and it worked, especially after what happened today."

"What happened today?" I asked.

"It doesn't matter anymore. You should forget about me and leave. I don't deserve your protection. I've faced a lot of shit in my life, and it made me strong. If I weren't on drugs again, I would've killed them all already instead of being a fucking victim. Now, if you want to help me," she took my hand and pleaded with her eyes. "They'll kill me when they're done. Whatever it is, you're all up to. I've seen their faces. I know who they are, and they know it. I'm a dead woman who happens to still be breathing."

It was the first time in my life that I wanted to do the absolute right thing. Maybe by saving this girl, I could atone for not saving Kiki and Helen.

"I want a reward," I said.

She lowered her eyes and then began to disrobe.

I stopped her hand.

"I don't want that. I want you to take me to Katerina. I've been looking for her all my life."

"But she's gone."

"Didn't she leave an address behind? Anything?"

"She told me she was going to the countryside. She sent a letter once. I might still have it at my place."

"Tell me where you live."

"I'm sorry, but I can't tell you that. Whatever you do to me, I'm not telling you where I live. I'd never feel safe in my own home."

"Where's your wallet, your ID?"

"You're wasting your time. My wallet's in the store in case someone looks for me. Please, just take me out of here, and I'll take you to my place. I must have her picture in my apartment. I will help you, and we will look together. But I can't stay here another night."

"I've looked for Katerina for so long. If there's an opportunity to find her, I wouldn't let it go. I'd risk everything to find her, even jail. But first, tell me what happened while I was away."

"Does it really matter?"

"It matters to me. I want a name or a description."

She lowered her head but remained silent.

"It was Stavros, wasn't it?"

"Please don't do anything. He told me that if I talk, he'll beat me worse the next time, and you can't always be around. Just get me out of here."

The main door opened. I couldn't show any signs of weakness. I whispered *sorry* to her, then fell on top of her, cursing and undressing her. To her surprise, she screamed.

Dimitris opened the door, and I slapped her. Dimitris grabbed me and yanked me off her.

"What the fuck are you doing? Are you trying to wake the whole neighborhood?"

"She was playing hard to get. Where are the others?"

"They're loading soil into the trucks. The job will be done on Monday or Tuesday. I was told to let you know. You mustn't leave your position at the bank. If you do another stupid thing like yesterday, you could burn us all."

"Okay, I get it. I'll go now. I need to go home, anyway."

I left without objecting to anything. I had to be alone to think. I decided to go home. On the bus, I saw a familiar face. Could he be the man my brother had assigned to watch me? I didn't like that at all. Was he following me beforehand? Did he know my previous moves?

If so, did he watch me enter Peter's house?

Could he hear the girl's screams?

How close to collapse was this gig?

Chapter 18

I WAS FINALLY HOME. I wanted to talk to Kostas this time, but he wasn't there. I had a quick shower and lay down. I had to go to bed and rest. Later, trying to wake up took great effort. My head felt like it would break, and my eyes stung. I took a painkiller and made coffee. Kostas was back. He sat speechless on the couch, watching me. I hadn't seen him, so it startled me when I turned and he was there.

"What business do you have with them?" he asked. "You know what kind of scumbags they are, don't you?"

"You've been watching me. Why?"

"Because I don't trust you. You will ruin my career. Imagine what will happen when you go to prison as a cop's brother. Some bad guys on the inside will think you're me."

Shit, I hadn't thought about that. Going to jail wasn't an option. Yet, if I told my brother the plan, I'd risk the girl's safety and never find Katerina. If I didn't tell him and they connected me to the bank robbery, I'd ruin him, which would kill him.

What had greater value? The girl's life? My life? My brother's life? Who would have thought that I'd be in such a horrible position? I wanted to do the right thing, but in this case, I had to decide which was best for everyone involved.

I sipped my coffee. "Kostas, I want you to know that no matter what happens, it's not my fault."

"Tell me what will happen. Open up to me for once. I am your brother, guardian angel, father, mother, and good self—we are one. Just talk to me. I beg you."

"You asking as my brother or a cop?"

"Your brother. I won't tell a soul, I promise. We'll work together to untangle the mess you're in. Trust me."

"If you don't speak up, you'll become an accomplice. Or you'll be accused of some form of a cover-up. I can't do that to you. I'll try to handle it myself, as I always do. If things get too tough, I'll ask for your help."

Kostas closed his eyes and leaned his head back as if he was exasperated.

I moved into the kitchen, quickly finished my coffee, and then slipped out the door without another word to my brother.

When I got to work, the van was outside the store beside the bank, and the lights were on. The team was hard at work. Several women walking the streets gazed at me strangely, a sure sign that the bald pimp had talked about me. I wanted to give him the information he was looking for. Maybe that way, I'd learn more about the girl back at Peter's place.

I wished there was a pill that removed certain memories so I could forget about Katerina.

I went to Peter's place as soon as my shift was over. I wanted to see her, listen to her. The others would continue the digging, and I would watch over her.

As soon as I entered the house, Peter was leaving her room. Behind him, I heard her screaming with rage.

"What happened?" I asked.

"Nothing. She begged me to release her, and I told her how the police would find her pieces scattered in the garbage." He laughed maniacally, placed a cigarette in his mouth, and stepped outside. I ran inside the room, and the girl gave me a stern look.

"I won't escape," she muttered. "Please, just hand me over to the police. I will say that you helped me. They won't be strict with you."

"Are you crazy? To the police?" I locked the door behind me and then approached her.

"Remember when I was beaten?" she whispered.

"Yes."

"I chewed through the rope that bound me. I ran outside, and Stavros caught me, beat me, and handcuffed me. He's the one who has the keys."

That was another problem I now had to solve. One set of handcuffs wasn't enough. He'd used two of them, one for each wrist. I hadn't noticed this detail before. I moved closer and hugged her as she was folded into the radiator next to her. Something about her reminded me of Helen.

"I'll help you," I whispered. "I just don't know how yet." Without realizing what I was doing, I kissed her on the mouth. A slow, wet kiss that made her shiver all over. I couldn't resist her. I started to caress her body. Although she was bound and beaten, I felt her body responding to my every move. She wanted me, and I wanted her. The attraction was powerful, and we were alone. Perhaps she was using me to help her, but I didn't mind. Sleep found us still embraced.

I woke abruptly in the middle of the night. I gently moved away from her. I couldn't understand why I felt so connected to her. Maybe it was the redemption of my soul after Helen. Perhaps I had replaced Helen with this girl. The one sure thing was that she had to be saved. I couldn't leave her fate in Peter's hands. My brother and I would find our way out of this alive, but this girl would surely be killed.

I got up and went to the living room so they wouldn't find me with her. I didn't want to show any sort of weakness. What I wanted to do was take the keys from Stavros. But could I do it on my own? I decided I needed an ally.

As soon as Peter came, I left in the early morning hours. I had to catch up with the pimp. I took a taxi and went there as fast as I could. This time, there was no one at the entrance of the strip club. I barged in and saw a lot of drunk men at the tables and a bunch of doped girls. The manager saw me and sent me to his boss.

The moment I stepped into his office, he offered me a blank stare.

"I told you I would bring you information," I said.

"Then talk."

"We had an agreement."

"I haven't forgotten about it."

"You were right. The earthworks thing going on beside the bank is just a cover-up."

"A cover-up for what?" I finally had his attention.

"A man named Stavros wants to steal your business. He's found girls and ready to put them in place. He's also found a few guys for protection. They're renovating the store for that business. The only thing I don't know is when he'll make his move."

"I will take them all out. Fuck that bastard. Who thinks he can take my place?" The pimp's eyes were shining. He stood up, the veins in his neck stretching.

"I will help you," I said. "I have more information. We can set it up quickly."

He lowered back to his chair. "Tell me what else you know."

"I know where they hang out. I can also find out when it will be best to catch Stavros off guard so you can take care of your business. Do whatever it is you want."

"Sounds good. What's in it for you?"

"The girl."

"What do you want to know about the girl?"

"I don't need to know anything about her right now."

He frowned. "So, what do you want then?"

"I want you to set her free. Stavros has imprisoned her at the house —I'll provide the location—to work for him as one of his bitches. I was looking for her, and when I couldn't find her, I approached you for help. However, I soon found out where she was being held, and now our deal became more important to me. I can't get to her alone, so I came to you to free this girl. Do we have an agreement?"

"What do you want her for?" He stared at me. "Why's she so important to you?"

"She owes money to a friend of mine. Take her out of the hole they put her in, and I'll take over from there. Do we have an agreement?"

He got up, walked around his desk, and offered me his dirty hand. I had managed to find a convincing lie to save the girl.

I left the strip club with several pounds of weight off my shoulders.

Stavros would be dealt with, and the girl would be saved.

Now I had to find my brother.

We had business of our own.

Chapter 19

I WENT HOME TO find Kostas getting ready to work.

"You look like shit," he said, putting on his jacket.

"Say one nice thing for once, damn it."

"Okay, how about, good morning. How are you?"

"Kostas." I glared at him. "We need to talk. Seriously."

"What's going on?"

"The time has come. I'm in trouble. It's a crazy entanglement."

"What happened? Tell me."

"I can't tell you yet."

"You just said we need to talk." He looked me in the eye, scared, about to lose his composure.

"If I tell you and you cover for me, I make you an accomplice. I can't do that to you. You're all I've got. It took you forever to pull yourself together. The last thing you need now is me and my decline."

"Stop preaching and just talk."

"I don't want you to question me. I want you to understand me."

"I don't want to interrogate you," he said. "I want to help you. Who will take care of you if you go to jail again?"

"It doesn't matter what will happen to me. I'm a burned soul that burns those who love me." I shook my head. "No, I can't tell you yet. Just stay out of it until I tell you."

"Tell me now."

"No, it's not possible yet. I'll let you know within a week. When the time's right, I'll need your help. Just trust me this once."

"Okay, brother, we'll do it your way." He placed a hand on my shoulder. "I knew something was wrong, even if you gave me excuses. I know you. I understand you like no one else." He hugged me then, and I felt tears rising.

"I know," I replied. It was the first time he hugged me like that and the last.

I never saw him again.

Two days passed, and I couldn't wait any longer. They were all so secretive, and I hadn't seen the girl, even though I'd wanted to. I didn't want them to be too suspicious. I believe that if they pressured her enough, she would talk about our conversations, so the best thing was to avoid her and go to my job like normal.

There were only a few days left to activate my plan, but it felt like months. They were all in the digging process, but Stavros guarded the girl twenty-four-seven. I was sure he was abusing her, but I couldn't do shit about it at that stage of the plan. If Peter made a phone call, she'd be dead, so it was better to wait.

During my evening shift, I did my job as I normally would. I entered the bank, did my regular rounds, logged my time through all the checkpoints, exited, and went home.

Tonight was calm and serene. The streets were eerily quiet—too quiet—without anything happening except internally. My heart pounded in my chest, my pulse raced, and breaths came in gasps. An icy cold gripped my body, and sweat rolled off my face. I grabbed a chair to keep from falling. I needed water. It wasn't the first time I had an anxiety attack. All this tension of how everything would eventually work out was taking a toll.

When I went inside the bank to perform a routine check, I heard a noise downstairs. I wasn't ready to look or deal with it as my heart hadn't slowed its racing. I collected myself, took two deep breaths, and slowly descended the stairs.

At first, I heard nothing new and was about to leave. I closed my eyes and listened again. Voices emanated from me. I quietly approached the area where the sounds were coming from, moving toward the vault and the lockers.

Then I saw their lookout.

"Quick, assholes, he'll be back in a while," someone said.

"Dimitris," someone else said. "Take as much cash as you can. Remember, we have to cover Stavros's share as well. I'm going to the lockers."

My team had lied to me.

They came in earlier than they had told me, and from an entrance, they hadn't told me about it.

There could only be one reason—to trap me, to let me take the fall.

They played me and made me think I was their partner. They had my fingerprints all over the house. The blame would fall on me for everything. My patrols covered the noise they made during the operation, and then they'd go quiet. They would be long gone by the time I'd figured out what had happened.

Peter used me.

And now he had to die.

I didn't have a registered gun but carried one with me anyway. I didn't care about anything anymore. I would just kill Peter and fuck everything.

I was done. Revenge was all I sought.

With my gun ready, I stepped out in front of them.

First, I shot one of the brothers, Dimitris, in the head. He dropped like dead weight.

Startled, they all drew their weapons. I fired wildly. I wasn't interested in what would happen, who would be killed, and who wouldn't. The other brother took a bullet in the chest and dropped hard on top of Dimitris. Blood splashed everywhere like someone was creating an artistic rendition of death.

Kyriakos held Dimitris's body while firing at me. I crouched to avoid being hit by gunfire, then hid behind a door.

"Come on, man," Peter shouted at me. "Stop firing at us. We can share everything."

I wanted him dead so badly. To drain every bit of life from inside him, every breath.

"Leave the money and go," I shouted at him.

"You know I won't do that. We came here with a purpose. And now we have more money to share. Maybe that's the way things were supposed to happen. Come with us to finish the job. Kyriakos, don't shoot at him."

"And Kyriakos? Didn't he come for money?"

"No, he cares about the secrets hidden in the lockers. Get out."

"Not while you're holding a gun."

"Okay. Kyriakos, throw your gun."

Peter nodded at Kyriakos to play along while he still held his gun. He needed me to be on their side. Otherwise, I'd notify the police, and they wouldn't get too far.

I came out of hiding, my gun held high, aimed at Peter.

He smiled. "Put down your weapon."

I pretended to lower it but then raised it and fired. I shot Peter in the eye. A splatter of blood crossed his face, and he fell back.

Kyriakos scrambled to get his weapon. He rolled on the floor, aimed, and shot me in the shoulder.

Hatred and anger coursed through me, turning me into a machine.

Kyriakos grabbed the first bag of money he saw and ran for the exit.

I approached Peter's body. Then I lowered to my knees and punched him in the face repeatedly. My hands were covered in blood. In front of me, when I looked at Peter, I saw all those who came before him, who had used me and hurt me. Takis, Mrs. Cleo, the reformatory bums, Peter with his gang, Stavros, and I punched them all as Peter's face turned to mush. After a while, the man before me wasn't recognizable. He no longer had a face.

I took one of the bags of money and searched for the entrance. I found the tunnel and went through it to the store. In the light, I realized I was covered in blood. I slid on a jacket to cover my shoulder wound. It probably looked like I'd just exited a slaughterhouse.

I found a phone booth and called the bald guy about Lisa. After that, my second phone call was to the police. I told them who I was, to warn my brother, and that a robbery occurred in the bank.

After hanging up, I walked to the streetlight, waited for a random car to pull up, then opened the door and yanked the guy out by gunpoint. I stole his car to go and hide the money and then surrendered. I would go to my brother's police station. Maybe I would be treated differently there.

These are the last things I remember.

I hope the girl tied to a radiator with two sets of handcuffs was saved, and I pray Katerina has a good life somewhere. I wasn't born a murderer—an unfair life without love made me who I am.

Thank you for listening, whoever you are.

I desperately needed to tell someone. And if there's a God, I hope he was listening, too.

I'm sorry, and I just wish life could've been different.

I tried in the end. I really tried.

Forgive me.

Chapter 20

"Doctor, can't his condition be treated in some way?" Lisa glanced at the doctor as they proceeded along the hospital corridor.

"I'm sorry, miss. The fact that he lived so many years with the illusion—the delusion—that his brother is alive is a miracle. He managed to be almost functional, looking and acting like a regular person. Who knows how many more people he had made up in his mind to survive? Of course, when confronted with the reality in the police station that day, no one could console him."

"When exactly did his brother die?"

"According to the information in his file, his brother died while being treated at the hospital for serious injuries from an explosion. He was in a coma that he never woke from, which some call a blessing due to what the flames had done to his body. He would've dealt with incredible pain for years to come." The doctor looked over at her. "He was a hero, too, as I understand it. Kostas was injured on duty."

"Can I see Nikos?"

"Only for a while. He's restrained to the bed by leather straps for security, so don't get upset. When he puts the people taking care of him in danger, we must take all the necessary precautions."

"I see," Lisa said as the doctor led her to Nikos's room and opened the door. Somehow, he'd managed to knock the bed over. She found him whispering in the corner, aimed toward the wall, his hands still tied to the bed. She eased closer and detected some of his final words.

"Forgive me. Goodbye, my friend. I feel much better now, but my time has come. If you ever find Katerina, tell her I love her and never stop looking for her."

Nikos spun around and began to shout, yanking on his restraints. The doctor called for help, and two nurses came. They could calm him down with great effort while he fought them and shouted, cursing with all his might. Some sedative was injected into his leg.

"As soon as my brother gets here, you will curse the moment you touched me."

Lisa stepped outside the room and watched through a window as they struggled with Nikos. He hadn't seen her, or he hadn't recognized her. Lost in his mind, he had no idea of his environment.

"Kiki, Kiki, don't leave," he shouted when he noticed her watching.

In Lisa's place, he was seeing his mother. She couldn't face any more of this today. She had already gone through a lot in her life. She slipped outside, tears streaming down her face.

Every opportunity in her life had faded. It no longer made sense to live. Nikos had lost his mind just when she understood how much she loved him.

She took a taxi to the abandoned maternity hospital where Nikos had spent his early years. The big iron door was wide open—someone had broken in. Now that the hospital had closed, it was a hangout for junkies and homeless people without hope.

She entered the courtyard where the patients had once walked. The fresh air always made her feel better. Of course, everything that had happened to her started in her childhood—her life was full of scars.

Her father had been a violent alcoholic, and her mother was missing. Her grandmother had tried to take her mother's place, doing her best to make her a strong grown-up. Her dad got involved with all the wrong people, and her grandmother had taken her away to keep her safe. She did whatever job she could find.

However, one day, her father came to see her. He'd brought several friends with him that day. It was the first time he had been so kind to her. Of course, he had his reasons. He was never good to someone unless he wanted something from them. This particular time, it was her he needed.

A man with thick, curly hair stood over her. "You will go to the child's school we are discussing and become her friend. You are the right age. If you don't do that, your father, who owes us a lot of money, will leave this world. He has done so much for you, so now it's your turn to do something for him."

"But why?" she asked.

"My doll, don't ask that," her father said. "You don't want to know."

"Sit down, Theodore, since your daughter wants to know, let's tell her. The girl you're to befriend is the daughter of an informant. Once she learns to trust you, you'll steal an envelope inside her house."

"Me? Steal something?"

"We have no one else in your age group. No one will suspect you and your father owes us."

That's how it all started. She made the girl a friend, an excellent friend, in fact. She was an adorable and innocent girl who believed her father was a postman. It was a matter of time until she took the envelope, but the guy with the curly hair said he had no patience. He wanted to move to another plan, and the time was up. So he pressured her to organize a kidnapping, but Lisa wasn't made for that shit.

She told her friend the truth and worked with the girl's father. When the man with the curly hair realized this, he killed her father in front of her. The police arrived, and Lisa survived with only one bullet for her troubles.

After her hospitalization, the girl's father managed to get her into the witness protection program since he was an informant. Since she had saved his daughter, she was considered a witness. With a new name and tremendous guilt—she blamed herself for her father's murder—Lisa took the wrong path. Drugs of all kinds, relationships of all categories, all alone against the world.

In her suffering, she met a guy. A handsome guy with style and finesse. It was only a matter of time before she fell in love and became his puppet. She trusted him and told him everything—even her real name. Everything was going well with her new relationship, and her life seemed to be going in the right direction, but her boyfriend had other plans, though. He told her he found an old friend who could help them make money. Maybe that's what they needed to get the fuck out of there. He took advantage of her, kept her as a hostage, imprisoned and abused her. He put the whole team in his sick game, and she couldn't tell, drugged up as she was. She couldn't help Nikos, too, because Peter was so well-networked that he knew the whole damn world. Devil in the form of an angel.

He also knew Kyriakos, the curly-haired guy, the one who killed her father, the one who wanted to kill her, too. Tied to the radiator, he would surely kill her, a slow and torturous death.

Would she ever get to thank Nikos for saving her life? With her boyfriend, Peter, dead and Stavros watching over her, he would surely kill her when the bank robbery failed. But some bald guy showed up with his own crew, and after killing Stavros, they released her. The bald guy said Nikos told him about Stavros stepping in on his territory, and he couldn't let that happen.

Without Nikos, she would be dead. And then she'd figured

something out.

She realized that Nikos was not just any Nikos, but *her* Nikos. Her protector in the maternity ward when she was severely beaten up all those years ago. Her friend had tried to make her smile. Her childhood love hadn't worn out over time. Peter trapped him, the same man who had trapped them all.

She had planned everything in her mind. She would go to the police and testify that Peter was behind everything that Nikos had been forced to cooperate.

But none of that happened.

She walked a long way until she reached an abandoned house. She dug in a hiding place under a broken cupboard with her hands. After some time, she found a magic box, their box. As she opened it, she felt like the little girl playing with the twins that time back when there was a small amount of happiness in her.

Inside the box was a letter. Her hands trembling, she opened it, and with tears in her eyes, she began to read Nikos's words:

My dear Katerina,

I know that if you're alive, your steps will lead you here one day. I hope life is well for you and healed all the wounds in your soul when you were a little girl. If you're reading this, it means I failed to find you. I haven't stopped looking for you, but I can't find you anywhere. Do you even know that I still exist? Did you ever think of me?

I love you.

You are my only true, untouchable love. Nothing could erase you from me.

If you search inside the wall, you will find gold plates and cash. I was collecting them for you. I don't need them, and I never needed them. They never brought me happiness. I'm a born loser. I have a life behind me full of mistakes and crimes. Now, I will surrender myself to the authorities. Maybe that way, I can save an innocent life and redeem myself that I never rescued you.

Don't try to look for me. I've lost all hope for happiness. I want you, though, to be well and happy. Wherever I am, whatever I do, you must know that I will love you to the last beat of my heart.

With infinite, endless love, Nikos.

The letter fell from her hands, and she burst into tears.

"I didn't have the chance to tell him I was Katerina. Maybe someday I will."

Afterword

Dear reader,

I hope you enjoyed reading *What He Didn't Know* as much as I enjoyed writing it.

The tragic lives of criminals in Greece inspired me to write a story on how the environment and someone's past can change the course of their life. There's a reason for everything people do unless they suffer from a serious mental illness. For example, if Nikos had a loving mother, he may not have turned out as he did. If Kiki had a caring father, perhaps she wouldn't have trusted the first man she fell in love with, and if Katerina had a family, maybe she wouldn't be controlled by someone like Peter, and on and on it goes.

There are so many ifs in every story that we forget to think of the reason behind someone's behavior, and that's the backbone of this novel. Everybody's got a story, and until we walk in their shoes and see the world through their eyes, we'll never know what they've gone through or why they do what they do—even things that we deem wild, weird, or crazy.

Less judging causes more understanding. More understanding creates more love and empathy. And with that, there'll be fewer of us walking around unjustified.

I want to thank my editor and international bestselling author, Jonas Saul, for believing in me more than anyone else.

And above all, I want to thank you, the reader. I'm eternally grateful.

Until next time, take care of yourselves and keep reading.

Yours,

Rania Stone

Also by Rania Stone

Rania Stone Titles

Novels

What He Didn't Know (Translated to English)
The Lives Between Us (Translated to English)
There Will Be Blood (Co-written with Jonas Saul)
The Soulless (Co-written with Jonas Saul)

Children's Books (All in Greek)

A Walk In The Garbage City
The Magic Ring
The War Of Fire And Water Drops
The Well Of Colors
Adventures In Bunny Land
Adventures In Bunny Land 2
Melina And The 100 Princesses

Rania Stone

The Cursed Chest
The Christmas Reindeer
Melinda And The Magical Crystal Ball
Cat-Tales

About Rania Stone

About Rania Stone

Rania Stone is the author of five adult novels and eleven children's stories. She's a well-known author in Greece and has recently had several novels translated into English. Her first English release, *What He Didn't Know*, came out in late 2020.

She's been writing for two decades and calls Greece her home.

Contact Rania Stone
Website: www.raniastone.com
Facebook: RaniaStone/Facebook
Bookbub: Rania Stone
Email: contact@raniastone.com
Instagram: Rania/Instagram